UNDERCOVER BILLIONAIRE

AMY ANDREWS

B
Boldwood

First published in Great Britain in 2025 by Boldwood Books Ltd.

Copyright © Amy Andrews, 2025

Cover Design by Colin Thomas

Cover Images: Colin Thomas and iStock

The moral right of Amy Andrews to be identified as the author of this work has been asserted in accordance with the Copyright, Designs and Patents Act 1988.

All rights reserved. No part of this book may be reproduced in any form or by any electronic or mechanical means, including information storage and retrieval systems, without written permission from the author, except for the use of brief quotations in a book review. This book is a work of fiction and, except in the case of historical fact, any resemblance to actual persons, living or dead, is purely coincidental.

Every effort has been made to obtain the necessary permissions with reference to copyright material, both illustrative and quoted. We apologise for any omissions in this respect and will be pleased to make the appropriate acknowledgements in any future edition.

A CIP catalogue record for this book is available from the British Library.

Paperback ISBN 978-1-83617-952-8

Large Print ISBN 978-1-83617-953-5

Hardback ISBN 978-1-83617-951-1

Ebook ISBN 978-1-83617-954-2

Kindle ISBN 978-1-83617-955-9

Audio CD ISBN 978-1-83617-946-7

MP3 CD ISBN 978-1-83617-947-4

Digital audio download ISBN 978-1-83617-948-1

This book is printed on certified sustainable paper. Boldwood Books is dedicated to putting sustainability at the heart of our business. For more information please visit https://www.boldwoodbooks.com/about-us/sustainability/

Boldwood Books Ltd, 23 Bowerdean Street, London, SW6 3TN

www.boldwoodbooks.com

*To Megan Haslam, who saw this book for the first time five years ago. I'm so glad we finally get to publish it together.
All good things come to those who wait.*

TRIGGER WARNING

Undercover Billionaire includes a brief, non-graphic scene depicting sexual assault in the work place involving secondary characters. Readers who may be sensitive to these elements, please take note.

1

Fuck! People. *So many damn people.* Happy, smiling, selfie-clicking people. Loud T-shirts and flip-flop people. Floral swimsuits and Speedos people.

Too much cleavage. *Way* too much c*ock*age.

And not even the nearby tray full of frothy drinks with bright red cherries could make up for the fact that Aristotle Callisthenes – or Ari George for the next week, anyway – was stuck with three thousand *people* for the next seven days and nights.

On a boat. In the middle of the Mediterranean. Where his ability to get away was severely hampered.

Dull pain from an encroaching headache gnawed at his temples. Ari didn't *do* people. Sure, most days of his life he *had* to interact with them, but it just wasn't his forte. Give him numbers and spreadsheets any time!

Only seven more days... *Christe!*

He plonked his ass on the bar seat. 'Whisky,' he said, barely looking at the approaching waitress as he slid his hand over the wood grain checking for stickiness. 'Neat.'

'That's a pretty serious drink for not even half past eleven in the morning.'

Ari glanced up to find a pair of pale green eyes sparkling at him above a little snub nose and a wide mouth turned upwards at the corners. The top lip was dominated by a fascinating Cupid's bow. The kind that invited licking. The kind he might have found irresistible once upon a time.

In a galaxy far, far away.

Her blonde hair was caught back in some kind of side ponytail thingy, leaving her long bangs loose around her oval face. He judged her to be in her mid to late twenties and, in the bright red of her *Hellenic Spirit* polo shirt, she looked the quintessential girl next door.

His gaze dropped to her nametag. *Kelsey*. Yep. She looked like a Kelsey. All sunny and bright and impossibly perky and it had nothing to do with her cup size, although, curiously, he *had* noticed the V of her cleavage.

The gnaw in his temples upsized to a throb.

Ari wanted to say, *That's me, Mr Serious*. But he didn't. *Smile. Flirt. Be friendly. Don't scare the fucking staff.* His brother's strict instructions rang in his ears. Theo always had been a pain in the ass.

Have some goddamn fun for a change.

Ari shrugged and forced a smile. The muscles of his cheeks, unused to the exercise, protested the movement. 'It's five o'clock somewhere, right?'

Kelsey laughed as she poured the whisky and Ari blinked at the sexy vibrato as it fluttered around him like confetti. It'd been a long time since any kind of laughter had penetrated the thick hide of his self-imposed isolation.

Kelsey looked like she knew how to have fun.

'It's 9 p.m. in Sydney.' She placed the glass on the bar. 'So it definitely needs one of these.'

She opened a blue paper cocktail umbrella and inserted it at a jaunty angle into his drink. She leaned back, admiring her handiwork, and laughed again, louder this time. Whisky with a cocktail umbrella looked utterly ridiculous but Ari found himself smiling despite the absurdity.

A different throb this time sliced between his ribs. Quickly, he picked up the glass, tossed the umbrella aside and threw the contents down. Placing the tumbler back on the bar, he said, 'Hit me, again.'

Whisky was the worst possible thing he could be ingesting in the face of his threatening migraine. But that was why God had invented pharmaceutical companies.

The blonde quirked an eyebrow slightly before pouring a second helping. Ari drained the glass and set it down. Kelsey lifted the bottle but he shook his head.

The ship horn sounded and people whooped and cheered and headed for the railings as the oldest ship in the Ōceanós cruise line pulled out of Civitavecchia. Beyond the reaches of the harbour, April sunshine threw diamonds at the sapphire blue of the Med.

Out there, the Greek Islands beckoned. Venice beckoned.

Ari glanced at his watch. Eleven thirty on the dot. 'You're Australian?'

'Good guess.'

Ari shrugged. He'd been born in Athens, raised in France, holidayed all over Europe and schooled in England. Accents were second nature. 'You're a long way from home.'

'I am indeed.'

'How long have you worked on cruise ships?'

'Seven years.'

'You like it?'

She smiled and tipped her chin at the view. 'I'm in the Mediterranean. What's not to like?'

Which was a good response, but didn't really answer the question, and if the need to medicate himself wasn't becoming increasingly urgent, he might have stuck around to probe some more. He pulled out his wallet. 'How much do I owe?'

'Oh, no, sir.' She shook her head. 'I'll just swipe the card you were given on check-in.'

'Oh yes, right.' Ari removed the card and deliberately placed his wallet on the bar top. 'Sorry. I forgot.'

'No worries.' She gave a teasing laugh. 'Your first time?'

It wasn't. Ari had been seven the day his grandfather had smashed a bottle of champagne against the bow of this very ship, launching it on its maiden voyage. He'd lost count of the number of cruise ships he'd travelled on since.

Smile. Flirt. Be friendly.

'Yep. Cruise virgin I'm afraid.'

The lie slipped smoothly from his tongue. He had a job to do and zero problem with pretending to be someone else to get it done. But her eyes lit playfully and Ari's heart skipped a beat.

'In that case,' she said, handing back his card, 'we'll be gentle with you, sir.'

She laughed at her joke and it was infectious, a smile spreading across Ari's face before he even registered what was happening. He wondered if his cheek muscles were as confused as he was about the situation. But it was hard *not* to smile, not to respond to her easy laughter and her light, flirty chatter.

The kind of flirty chatter he suspected she used with *everyone* regardless of age or sex. It obviously came as naturally as breathing and he envied her that lightness of spirit.

Ari suddenly felt ancient at the grand age of thirty-two.

Smile. Flirt. Be friendly.

But he couldn't. His temples throbbed, the pain in his ribs was back, his breath was short. His smile faded and he stood to go, and instead of saying something like *Don't be gentle on my account*, which was something the old Ari might have said, he bade her goodbye.

Then he left, dodging *all the fucking people* and not stopping until he reached the dark, private cocoon of his inside cabin.

* * *

'Well, hello there. This is my lucky day.'

Kelsey glanced up from the drink she was pouring to find Andy, her fellow bartender, brandishing a wallet. She recognised it immediately as belonging to Whisky Dude.

She handed the drink over to her customer as Andy strode around the corner, out of sight. Hurriedly, she scanned the passenger's card and was grateful that people were still absorbed with getting underway. In a few minutes they'd be slammed by passengers wanting booze to celebrate their departure, but for now, she could go and check on her partner.

Kelsey had mixed feelings about Andy. She'd worked with him on and off the last two years and had even fooled around with him once at a party in the staff quarters on their first cruise together. He was English, four years younger than her twenty-seven years and a good kisser. But his moral code was a bit on the lax side. A fact confirmed when she found him rifling through the wallet.

'Two condoms and two hundred and twenty euros.' He waved the notes in the air. 'A tip for me *and* you,' he said with a wink. Kelsey was sure he was joking but she wasn't laughing.

'Very funny.' She snatched the wallet and held out her other hand. 'Give it back.'

'Oh, come on, Kels, he won't miss a couple of twenties. He probably won't even know.'

Silently, she stared Andy down. A couple of hundred euros was hardly a fortune – but *she'd* know if some of it was missing.

She'd bet Whisky Dude would, too.

Those dark eyes of his had been steady and intense, appraising her face with an attention to detail that had caused a little flutter in her chest. She doubted he missed a single goddamn thing. Not to mention, as the senior staff member, it'd be her ass if the passenger made a complaint.

God knew she couldn't afford to lose her job. Not now. Not when she was just one more year from her goal.

'*I'll* know.'

He sighed as he handed over the cash. 'You are a spoilsport, Kelsey Armitage.'

She nodded. 'Atta boy.'

* * *

Four hours later, her shift over, Kelsey made her way to Ari George's room on deck seven, his wallet in her hand. A couple of keystrokes of the register and she'd been able to access his name and room number from the card he'd given her to swipe. And other information. Like there being no Mrs George.

Or any other companion…

No wedding band either, she'd noticed. Or a telltale white line where one would be if he was that kind of scumbag.

Of course, none of those things meant he wasn't in a relationship. But it was rare to see an attached man going solo on a cruise. Most men either travelled with their partners or they were a younger crowd travelling in groups looking to get drunk and laid.

She should just have handed the wallet to guest services – it was protocol, after all. But she hadn't been able to stop thinking about the man at her bar drinking whisky at eleven in the morning.

Or his brooding good looks.

The intensity of his obsidian stare, the thickness of his lashes, the squareness of his ruthlessly shaved jaw line, the perfect straightness of his nose, the hollows beneath the twin rails of his cheekbones, the firm line of his mouth.

The deep, lurking… sadness in his eyes.

She'd always been a sucker for sad eyes. Which was probably why she was here, at a passenger's cabin, breaking all the rules, delivering the abandoned wallet personally.

He probably wasn't even *in* his cabin. It was three thirty in the afternoon on a gorgeous day, the sun was shining and the Med was being its beguiling self. Surely no one in their right mind *would* be indoors?

In which case, she'd find the room attendant, get the door opened and leave it on his bed. She'd swiped a cocktail umbrella from the bar to use as a calling card for such an eventuality and her lips curved at the thought of him finding the little yellow umbrella atop his wallet.

At the thought of him knowing *she'd* left it on his bed.

Kelsey stared at his door, hesitating. Maybe she should just give it to the attendant and let them deal with the situation. She looked over her shoulder – the hallway was empty. *Screw it*. She'd knock, and if he didn't answer, she'd go to plan B.

With her pulse washing through her ears, Kelsey rapped on the door. A muffled 'Just a moment' caused a hitch in her breath as the reality of seeing him again gripped her chest.

It was utterly preposterous – he was just a man, for fuck's sake. And a *passenger* at that!

Which did not prepare her – one iota – for the sight that greeted her as the door opened. Not for his wild bed hair or the dark shadow of his whiskers or the pillow mark on his face. Not for him to be dressed in nothing but a towel or the way he appeared to be trying to focus.

Was he... drunk?

Had he continued the whisky party in his cabin? He didn't smell boozy but hell, it was so dark behind him he could be concealing a drug den for all she could tell.

'Oh, hey.' He frowned, his hand going to the knot of the towel sitting snug and low on narrow hips.

The action pulled her gaze downwards. Over the broad span of his shoulders and the smooth bronzed planes of pecs dusted in a light covering of hair, down the furrow bisecting his firm abs, and lower still to the happy trail heading south from his belly button.

'Sorry,' he said, his voice gravelly.

A hint of an accent she hadn't picked up earlier roughed up his smooth English enunciation.

Italian? Greek?

'I thought you were room service.'

Kelsey dragged her gaze upwards as he shoved a hand through his hair. The action bunched his triceps and revealed a dark thatch of hair under his arm that was masculine as fuck and caused a riot in her underwear.

She blinked. What the hell? Since when had *armpits* been a turn on? Because she was most definitely turned on by this long, lean hunk of a man. It may have been a while but she knew chemistry when it reached out and tweaked her nipples.

'No, I came to...' She held up his wallet. 'You left this behind.'

He frowned again. 'Oh right, thanks.'

He reached for it but swayed alarmingly and, before she could check the impulse, Kelsey slid her hand onto his forearm. It was warm and hard, the dark hair springy beneath her palm.

'Whoa. Are you okay? Are you sick?' She peered into his face as he shut his eyes and leaned heavily into the door. 'I could call the ship doctor?'

His eyes blinked open and, between their intense focus and the heat of his skin, Kelsey could barely breathe. A lock of his hair had fallen forward onto his forehead into an honest-to-God curl, and her palm itched to push it back.

'I'm fine,' he dismissed. 'I'm just coming out of a migraine. I'm always a bit lightheaded afterwards.'

'Oh God, I'm sorry. My mother suffers from them. Is there anything I can do? A cold compress, a drink of water, some tea?'

'Room service is bringing peppermint tea.'

Kelsey would have sworn Mr Whisky would be a coffee man. That strong, bitter shit that caused a jolt to the heart at the first sip. Tea sounded so... English. But then, so did he.

Mostly.

'I just need to sit.'

Not trusting his ability to stay upright, Kelsey followed Ari into his cabin, lowering herself down beside him on the bed as the door clicked shut. The cabin plunged into a darkness that was the hallmark of inner cabins on cruise ships.

'How's that?' Kelsey asked into a silence exacerbated by the deep, bottomless black hole pressing in from all directions.

She should take her hand off him, but he felt solid and real as her eyes adjusted to the tomb-like gloom. His aftershave seemed more pronounced too. *Sweet.* Wrapping her in a cloud of maple syrup and a fuck-ton of pheromones.

He grunted. 'Better.'

'Is it okay if I turn on the lamp or do you still need it off?' Kelsey's mother needed the dark when she was in the grip of a migraine.

'On is fine.'

The low rumble of his voice went straight to her nipples and Kelsey was momentarily thankful for the lack of light as she inched her way around the bed, his wallet still in her hand. Her feet found what she assumed were his clothes discarded on the floor. She resolutely ignored them – the less she thought about how little he was wearing, the better!

She continued on until her knee bumped the bedside table. Placing the wallet down, she groped for the lamp switch and flicked it on, immediately adjusting the dimmer switch at the base. A low, yellow glow, like a single candle flame, illuminated the cabin.

Kelsey glanced over her shoulder, noting the sheets had been pulled back before her gaze snagged on the golden play of light across the planes and angles of his back and shoulders. His hair was short at the nape, which only seemed to emphasise the riot of dark waves atop his head.

'That okay?' she asked quietly.

He nodded. 'Thank you.'

A knock and a murmured 'Room service' startled Kelsey.

He started to rise but she waved him down. 'I'll get it,' she said, hurrying to the door, pleased he didn't try to pull some bullshit macho act about being okay.

Kelsey hadn't really thought about who might be on the other side and whether she'd know them but, thankfully, she didn't. On a ship with a thousand-plus staff and a turnover higher than any ship she'd ever worked on, it wasn't uncommon.

But Kelsey was still in the red shirt and white knee-length shorts worn by the staff manning the pool deck bar, which could be problematic if the room service attendant was a stickler for rules. Thankfully, he didn't appear to pay Kelsey any attention and was happy to hand the tray over and depart.

Placing the tray on the nearby desk, beside a closed laptop, Kelsey fussed around making his tea, adding the cocktail umbrella on the spur of the moment. It looked even more ridiculous in a cup of tea, but she remembered how he'd smiled at the one she'd put in his whisky, and maybe a little comic relief wouldn't go astray right now?

Sitting beside him again, she offered him the cup and saucer. He gave a barely-there smile. 'Do you walk around with a supply of them?'

'Tools of the trade.'

He took the cup off the saucer, placed the umbrella on it and sipped at his tea in silence for a long moment. Heat radiated from his body, and Kelsey was conscious of how close they were as the peppermint from his tea joined the bouquet of aromas playing havoc with her senses.

'Do you get them very often?' Her voice was tentative as it broke the silence.

He cradled the cup in his lap. 'I used to, not so much any more.'

'Have you had them investigated? Sometimes they're more than just a headache, you know?'

As soon as the words were out, Kelsey wanted to bite her tongue. *Nice one, Kels. Why not imply the man has a brain tumour?*

'I mean... I didn't mean anything serious like a...' *Bloody hell, don't say the T word!* 'It could just be you need... glasses or something simple.'

Oh, Jesus. Shut up already!

His black eyes sought and held hers for a moment and then he chuckled, his beautiful mouth parting. Kelsey blinked as the noise poured over her skin like warm oil. Sadly, it didn't last.

'I was in an accident three years ago. It's a residual thing from that.'

'Oh God, I'm sorry. Were you badly hurt?'

'Not really.' He stared into his tea. 'I was lucky.'

He raised the cup to his lips, obscuring half his face but not the trace of bitterness that had laced the word 'lucky'. It was stark in the profound silence. Clearly, there was more to that story.

Was that why his eyes were so sad?

She inspected his profile as he drank, looking for answers, but his face was a mask. And it wasn't any of her business. He was a *passenger,* for fuck's sake. She'd returned his wallet and helped him out when he'd been unwell. She'd fulfilled her duties as a member of the *Hellenic Spirit*'s crew.

Gold star for her. Now get out!

'Well...' She placed the umbrella on the tea tray and handed him the empty saucer. 'I best be off, if you're sure you're okay.'

The teacup rattled against the saucer. Those dark eyes slid once again to hers and locked tight. 'Yes, thank you.' His gaze slipped to her mouth with a laser-like focus.

Kelsey suddenly realised how close they were, their arms and thighs only inches apart. Her breath hitched and her hand shook a little as she concentrated on inhaling. She'd been with guys who could excite her with a look but never with one who could interfere with her ability to breathe.

Who made her feel like there wasn't enough air.

'It wasn't any trouble.'

Her voice sounded weird. High and strange, like she'd been sucking on helium. Not the usual husky quality. And still, he stared at her mouth, and every pulse point in Kelsey's body started to throb. Her nipples hardened.

Her belly tightened. Heat radiated from his thigh to hers, sliding up her leg. All the way up.

She really, *really* should leave.

'Maybe,' he murmured. 'Still...'

Kelsey waited for him to continue, to finish what he'd been about to say, but he didn't. He just kept staring at her mouth, the sound of his breathing growing rougher and rougher, thicker and thicker, until it rubbed against her exposed flesh like a velvet glove.

He kissed her then, his mouth swift as it breached the distance between them, his lips pressed hot against hers. Not moving, just pressing. Not hard but not light either.

Firm.

Pressing and pressing. Not opening or shifting to take the kiss deeper. Not attempting to touch her. Just pressing. And breathing – hard and fast. Sucking air in and out of his nostrils in swift, harsh respirations, like he was struggling to keep himself in check.

Or struggling against some kind of internal demons.

Kelsey's pulse hammered at her temples and beat a wild tango between her legs as she tried to compute myriad sensations coursing through her body. How perfectly his mouth fitted against hers, how her erogenous zones had lit up like a pinball machine, how his loud, crazy breathing was a bigger turn on than everything else put together.

How she was kissing a virtual stranger. A near-naked virtual stranger. In his cabin. At her work.

A *passenger*.

Her sex tingled and her body pulsed at a primal level. The kind that made a lot of women stupid.

But Kelsey had used up her quota of stupid.

Tearing her mouth away, she jumped to her feet, stumbling back two steps, dragging in oxygen. 'I... can't,' she muttered.

'*Christe!*' He shoved a hand in his hair as he stood, placing the cup and saucer on the tray before holding up his hands in a placatory manner. 'I'm sorry.'

Kelsey shook her head, a wild unchecked thrill zinging through her body at the sight of his big, almost-naked body. 'It's against the rules to...'

Fuck the passengers was what she wanted to say, because God knew she wanted to push Ari George onto his bed and ride him like a pogo stick.

'We're not supposed to fraternise.'

'Of course. *Theé*. Of course.'

Christe... Theé... Kelsey realised absently the passenger she'd just gotten *waaay* too close to was Greek.

'Please, forgive me,' he continued. 'I... don't know what came over me. It was *unforgiveable*.'

He shoved his hands on his hips, drawing her gaze downwards again. To what lay under the towel. The light might have been low but there was no mistaking the state of his arousal or the fact the man was packing some serious dick.

'I don't do this,' she said, dragging her gaze back to his face. Kelsey wasn't a rule breaker. And she needed this job. She had financial responsibilities. 'Some staff do cross that line, but not me. I've *never* done this.'

She had no idea why she felt the need to convince him. Given *he'd* kissed *her*, she didn't think he'd report the incident. Maybe she was just trying to convince herself? Convince her body it didn't need what he had under that towel.

'I believe you,' he said as he sunk down on the bed behind him. 'It wasn't your fault. It was mine.' He propped his elbows on his knees, leaned forward at the hips and cradled his face into his palms. 'You should go.'

If Kelsey had been in her right mind, his dismissal might have rankled. Right now, she was glad for the out as she turned on her heel and fled the cabin.

2

Ari woke several hours later to pitch black. Momentarily disorientated, the slight fuzziness behind his eyes reminded him of his migraine and the rest came flooding back.

Kelsey. The wallet. The kiss...

Groping for the light switch, he flicked it on, shutting his eyes against the intrusion even though it was still only the dim glow from earlier. Opening his eyes, he let his vision adjust before rolling his head to the side, his gaze falling on the yellow cocktail umbrella sitting next to his wallet.

He'd grabbed it up on his way back to bed and placed it on the bedside table, its paper canopy open wide and almost transparent. He picked it up again now, twirling it slowly, smiling as he remembered Kelsey.

Normally, he'd see something like this and think of Talia. But not now. He wasn't thinking about his dead wife right now; he was thinking about the woman who had decorated both his whisky glass and his teacup with a bright bit of kitsch, her green eyes dancing.

And that felt all kinds of wrong. The umbrella was a ridiculous piece of... whimsy, and it shouldn't be making him smile. He'd kissed *another woman* – that should be making him ill. The first woman since his wife had died.

Well, technically not the first.

He *had* picked up a woman in the bar of his Edinburgh conference hotel and gone back to her room two months after Talia's death. But that had been a desperate attempt to think about something – *anything* – other than his crushing loss, and he hadn't exactly crowned himself in glory.

Despite wanting – *needing* – to forget about Talia for just a little while, he hadn't been able to go through with it. She hadn't smelled the same or felt the same and Ari had realised he wasn't forgetting, he was *pretending*, and that wasn't fair to the poor woman who'd put herself out there. He'd left the room, disgusted with himself, and checked out of the hotel immediately.

But what had happened with Kelsey earlier was worse. Because he hadn't really wanted the woman in Edinburgh, but he *had* wanted Kelsey.

And that was like a hot fist to his gut.

Maybe this was that moment people – the therapist he'd seen for a while and well-meaning friends and family – talked about. The 'time heals all wounds' moment. Because he hadn't thought once about Talia. Not when he'd invited Kelsey into the room, not when she'd sat on the bed beside him, not when the urge to kiss her had come over him.

Not when he *had* kissed her.

Ari twirled the umbrella absently as he relived the moment again. He'd kissed her. *He'd* kissed *her*.

Even now, he couldn't say what had come over him, but his pulse had rushed through his ears and his chest had filled with the burning need to taste her mouth, and suddenly his lips were landing on hers and it had been such a shock he'd been too stunned to move.

He hadn't ever thought this moment would come. The moment he'd desire another woman. He hadn't sought it or expected it. In fact, he'd been *just fine* without that aspect in his life.

He'd been content knowing he'd had his one great love.

But here it was – *desire* – and Ari didn't know what to do with it. How could something he didn't need or want feel so good? How had the physical pain he'd felt sitting at the bar over his unexpected reaction to Kelsey's perky friendliness have melted away so easily when they were sitting on his bed?

Because it *had* been... easy. So easy.

Ari's heart seized in his chest at the thought, and he tossed the umbrella in the bedside bin as if it had suddenly turned into a live snake. He wasn't ready for that – to move on. He still felt... married. Logically, he knew he wasn't being unfaithful to Talia, but he wasn't ready to *replace* her, either.

Theo would be over the moon if he knew – not that Ari would ever disclose what had happened. But his family had been shoving women at him for the last two years, hoping they'd be some kind of antidote to his grief.

Ari understood they were worried about him, concerned about his reclusiveness and fretting about how he'd withdrawn into his job, how he'd buried himself in numbers and spreadsheets instead of facing *life*. But they'd been his salvation during his blackest, bleakest days.

Being productive, taking over the reigns as the Ōceanós Line CFO to drag the family's ailing cruise ship enterprise back into the black, had given him a reason to get up every morning.

A purpose.

Speaking of which, Ari checked his phone for the time. Almost seven o'clock. It wasn't surprising he'd slept for so long. Enduring a migraine was a physically exhausting experience for which sleep was the best cure.

And he *was* on holiday.

Well, *officially*, anyway. Unofficially, despite cocktail umbrellas and mind-bending kisses, Ari was here to do a job. He was on the *Hellenic Spirit undercover* to investigate why the ship that had once been the pride of the fleet was not only losing paying passengers and therefore money but also having difficulty retaining staff.

He'd suggested this scenario at the board meeting two weeks ago, assuming the company would employ someone to undertake the comprehensive clandestine assessment. After all, secret passengers, like secret shoppers, were tactics they'd employed before to assess passenger experience and keep crew on their toes.

But then Theo had suggested Ari be the one. Ari had protested – *all those fucking people* – but, as Theo had been quick to point out, no one would do a more thorough, more targeted assessment than Ari because nobody knew the business better or took more pride in the ships and their profitability than Ari.

Also, being the *other* Callisthenes son, the younger one – the one who *didn't* appear every other week on the cover of a tabloid magazine or revel in being an international playboy – he could blend in without being recognised.

Plus, you need a fucking holiday.

The board – which consisted entirely of family members from his grandfather to his parents and assorted uncles, aunts and cousins – had nodded their heads at Theo's irritable proclamation.

Ordinarily, Ari would have told Theo to go screw himself, board meeting or not, but his brother had known just the right strings to pull. The *Hellenic Spirit's* continued problems were a matter of personal pride for Ari. It was the only ship that hadn't shown improvement since the measures he'd put in place across the entire fleet when he'd become the CFO.

Staff turnover was high, customer satisfaction surveys were subpar and three out of the last dozen cruises had seen outbreaks of gastro bugs. Not to mention the steady decline in numbers, *this* voyage being no exception.

The *Hellenic Spirit's* capacity was four thousand people – two thousand three hundred passengers and seventeen hundred crew. There were currently fifteen hundred passengers on board. That was a shortfall of eight hundred guests, which was, in the long run, unsustainable.

And he – or Ari George, anyway – was here to uncover why.

Ari roused himself, swinging his legs over the side of the bed. He needed to get dressed for his seven thirty dinner sitting and then he was going to spend a few hours checking out the casino.

His gaze fell on the cocktail umbrella sitting in the bottom of the bin, and an image of Kelsey rose unbidden. A slug of grief, dark and visceral, hit him square in the middle of his sternum and he scrambled for his mental cache of Talia images. The one on their wedding day with her smiling up at him like he'd hung the goddamn moon offered itself up, and he grabbed on, refusing to relinquish it as he pulled his gaze from the bin.

Spotting his wallet, he reached for it, suddenly remembering he'd yet to check the contents. He'd deliberately left it behind to see if it was returned to him and if so, if anything was taken. He'd put in enough money to be tempting but not raise questions about his level of wealth.

He was supposed to be an ordinary Joe, after all – not a multi-millionaire heir to a Greek shipping line.

Ari counted the money. *Twice.* Two hundred euros. He counted it again. There was twenty missing. A feeling of dread sunk to the pit of his stomach and his throat went tight.

His *guilt* intensified.

Had Kelsey taken it? Had she come here, smiled at him, sat with him, brought a *fucking cocktail umbrella* with her all while *his* twenty burnt a hole in her pocket?

No. He *couldn't* believe she'd steal, that she was some kind of player. Ari was usually a very good judge of character and Kelsey had struck him as genuine right from the get-go. He couldn't believe it was her.

Which left a different scenario. A light-fingered passenger? The guy who'd been working the bar with her? Or another explanation? Ari made a note to check the CCTV footage at the end of the cruise. He'd left the wallet in plain sight so it should be easy to see who picked it up.

He just prayed like hell it wasn't Kelsey.

He'd looked up her staff record when he'd returned to the cabin. She was an excellent employee, with a clean record and a rapid career trajectory. The kind of staff they'd had difficulty retaining on this ship. They needed more Kelseys.

* * *

It was just after eleven when Kelsey made it back to the staff cabins. She'd worked the dining room from six until nine and the Aphrodite Lounge on deck fourteen for the last two hours. All she wanted was a shower and to hit the sack until she had to be up at five thirty for the 6 a.m. breakfast shift.

And a little alone time to think about her earlier transgression. With a *passenger*! God... what *had* she been thinking? Going into his cabin. Sitting on his bed.

Letting him kiss her.

But there was, as usual, a 'shoving off' party going on in the mess – a tradition for the first night of a cruise. Not that any of this lot needed an excuse to party. Put a thousand-plus mostly twenty-somethings in a room with cheap booze and it was *always* five o'clock.

'Kels!'

Tiffany, her best friend, waved at her from across the room. Also from Australia, they'd both been recruited to the Ōceanós family in the same intake and had largely worked the same Mediterranean cruises. But where Kelsey had grown up in a city, loved the beach and saw her job as a means to an end, Tiffany had grown up on a cattle property in the middle of nowhere and saw cruising as a grand adventure far, far away from the heat, dust and flies.

Tiffany was dark haired and curvy – big boned, as she like to call herself – and worked in the casino. At the blackjack table she was quiet and dignified, her hair pulled back into a sleek bun, her uniform fitting her like a glove. She was the whole *Casino-Royale*-elegant-sophisticated-croupier wet dream.

But out of her uniform and away from the tables, she held no airs and graces. She was just a sheila from the cattle station who could muster cows, fix a fence, string a bunch of swear words together that would make a cowboy blush and drink an SAS officer under the table. She also, genuinely, didn't give one fuck what people thought about her.

Kelsey loved her. *Everybody* loved her.

'Grab a beer,' Tiffany said, the quiet demure voice she used at the tables nowhere in sight. 'Join us.'

Kelsey nodded, resigning herself to one beer, and headed towards the bar. 'Hey, Sivat.' She greeted the Malaysian bartender warmly. He'd manned the staff bar on every one of her cruises. 'A beer please.'

'You look tired,' he said as he poured her drink. 'I thought you were quitting this crazy lifestyle?'

Kelsey laughed. 'One more year, Sivat, and I'm outta here.'

She'd have recouped enough of the money her ratfink ex had stolen – an *inheritance* from her grandmother – by then. Enough to put a deposit on the Pelican Cove beach cottage she and her mother had been coveting for what felt like a million years.

As Sivat handed the drink over, Andy sidled up and greeted her with a flirty smile.

'Hey,' Kelsey said.

'Returned the wallet, Ms Goody Goody?' he teased as he motioned to Sivat for a beer.

She rolled her eyes. 'Yes.'

'And was he grateful?'

Kelsey's mind strayed to the kiss even though she knew it hadn't been about the wallet. 'Yes. He was.'

'See.' Andy reached into his pocket and pulled out a twenty-euro note. 'I told you he wouldn't miss it.'

Kelsey stared at the note, dumbfounded for a moment, a hot cloud of *what-the-fuck* mushrooming in her chest. Her face flushed as her blood pressure rose. 'You're fucking kidding me.' She snatched the money out of his hand.

'Hey,' Andy protested.

'Are you out of your mind? I took his wallet to him personally,' she hissed. 'He's going to think I stole it.'

'All right, all right, don't get your panties in a tangle.'

Her blood pressure spiked. 'God, you can be such a *jerk*. You pull this shit again, I'm reporting you.' She thunked her undrunk beer down on the bar and stalked away.

* * *

Kelsey, who too often cursed the ridiculous enormity of cruise ships, was exceedingly thankful for the size of the ship tonight. She needed the time to cool down.

Did Ari know the money was missing? Had he noticed? And if so, had he reported it? Christ, she could lose her job over this! After seven years of hard graft and being away from home, she could lose it all over someone else's greed.

Sure, visiting a passenger's cabin, *kissing* a passenger, was also forbidden, but Kelsey wasn't really worried about the possibility of that coming out. *Stealing* from said passenger, though? That was a one-way ticket to the unemployment queue.

Fuck you very much, Andy!

Her pulse beat like a drum in sync with her step as she entered deck seven, the twenty in her hand hot and sweaty. And heavy. Like she was about to hand a guy she barely knew, who could shoot her career in the foot, a loaded gun.

Christ – what must he think of her?

She'd caught a glimpse of him tonight across the dining room as he'd been seated. He'd been hot as fuck in a suit and their eyes had locked and, for an awful second, Kelsey had realised the enormity of what she'd done. Of the line she'd crossed when she'd gone to his cabin and how vulnerable she'd made herself to consequences. She'd never felt as exposed as she had right there in the middle of that massive, elegant, two-level dining room.

And this from someone who'd been duped by a guy she'd *loved* who'd stolen all her inheritance money.

But then he'd glanced quickly away as if nothing had happened between them and, even as that felt kind of sickening, his pretence was far less of a risk to her job than his attention.

Thankfully, the passageway was deserted but the spectacular first night show in the Adelphi Theatre would be finished soon and the passageway would be full of people retiring to their cabins. Putting on a spurt of speed, she hurried to his door, her brain grappling with the looming conversation.

She'd been so ticked at Andy, she hadn't given any thought to what she'd say when he opened the door. *If* he opened the door. There were plenty of entertainment options on a ship this size which he could easily be out enjoying. A good-looking man like Ari would no doubt find easy companionship at any of the ship's venues.

That thought made Kelsey unaccountably twitchy, so her brain skipped to another possibility. What if he was asleep? And she was waking him to tell him *what* exactly? That her dickhead bartender partner had thought it'd be funny to steal from Ari?

Yeah... not that. *Definitely not that.*

Maybe she'd found it tonight around the back of the bar and thought it might be his? That could work.

Okay, so she'd knock lightly and if he didn't answer she'd hightail it out of here and try again tomorrow. Via a phone call. It was too risky coming to his cabin – again.

Kelsey knocked. It was quiet but would definitely be audible from inside the cabin. Hell, he could probably hear her heart knocking against her ribs from *inside* the cabin!

Inside...

How was it going to feel seeing him again in the same intimate surrounds as before? Especially given the last time she was here he'd kissed her and she hadn't been able to stop thinking about it since. About how close she'd come to surrendering and crossing a line she'd never crossed before.

Never been tempted to cross.

Oh God – a sudden thought occurred to her. What if he thought she was presenting for round two?

Alarmed, Kelsey turned to leave, but it was too late as the door opened abruptly. The lines she'd been rehearsing died on her lips at the sight of his naked chest. For the love of all that was holy – *again?* Did the man just strip off and walk around in his towel the second he got into his room?

His eyes widened a little as his gaze settled on her, his stance turning stiff. It reminded her of that brief, impersonal eye lock he'd spared her in the dining room. 'Oh. Hi.' His lips were kinda stiff too, drawing attention to his mouth and the dark shadow of his whiskers.

Crap. Not exactly pleased to see her. 'Hi,' she said and swallowed against the rapid thickening in her throat.

She heard voices from further down the passageway and quickly scanned over her shoulder to find a group of six elderly passengers all laughing and chatting, obviously on the way to their cabins. *Shit.* They couldn't see her face and they weren't paying her any heed, but she had zero desire to be recognised.

'Could I come in for a moment?'

If possible, he stiffened some more and the knuckles wrapped around the door handle blanched white. Jesus, did he really think she wanted to expose herself to any more potential reputational damage by being in his cabin? With him barely dressed again and given what had happened in there earlier?

But she was *not* going to have the money conversation with Ari standing in the passageway in her uniform.

'Please.'

Reluctantly, Ari fell back to make way for her and Kelsey stepped inside, brushing past him, noting the low glow from the bedside lamp was the only light in the cabin. As she drew to a halt at the foot of the bed, the door clicked shut and she turned to face him. His eyes met hers before they travelled down her body, heat building in his gaze as it took in her formal uniform of red button-up blouse and dark grey pencil skirt.

The air zinged suddenly as heat morphed to a raw kind of hunger. His body may have been putting out keep out signals, but his eyes were telling a different story. Her gaze zeroed in on the knot of that towel, and she blinked as a surge of lust flooded her pelvis.

Oh no. Down, girl – down! She was not here for this. It would not be sensible or practical and she was nothing if not sensible and practical.

Kelsey briefly shut her eyes to block the temptation of him. *Get your shit together, woman!* Opening her eyes, she held up the twenty-euro note in her hand. 'I found this—'

She stopped and cleared her throat. Her voice had gone all helium on her again, which sounded guilty as fuck. She *had not* taken the money and she would be damned if a wobbly voice said otherwise.

'In the bar tonight. It was on the floor out the back near where I'd looked through your wallet when I was trying to find who it belonged to.'

Kelsey fought against the urge to swallow – another sign of guilt – despite her throat being dry as day-old croutons. 'It must have fallen out and I didn't realise.'

He didn't say anything for the longest time, just looked at her, a frown creasing his brow as his gaze flicked from the money then back to her, his gaze probing. Assessing.

'Thank you.' He stepped closer until he was able to reach for the note, which he took out of her hand. 'I thought I'd had more money in my wallet but...' He shrugged. 'A migraine can often make me fuzzy about facts.'

So he *had* noticed. Was that why he'd been so stiff and unwelcoming just now? Why he hadn't acknowledged her at dinner tonight? Had he suspected her of taking it? And if so, why hadn't he reported it or made a complaint?

'I appreciate you returning it.'

'Of course,' she said, dismissing the gesture as a no-brainer with a quick shake of her head.

He stepped around her, the warm bulk of his bicep brushing hers. An army of goosebumps marched up her arm, across her chest and puckered her nipples. She caught a whiff of maple syrup again as he crossed to the bedside table, picked up his wallet and replaced the note.

Kelsey watched the shift and play of muscles beneath the burnished barrier of his skin, the clench of his ass beneath the towel. He turned and Kelsey quickly skittered her gaze to the left, although she was pretty damn sure he'd caught her perving.

'I—' She swallowed, her mouth far from dry now thanks to an excess of saliva, as she met his gaze. 'Better go.'

Two ink-black eyes drifted over her mouth, down her throat, to the open V of her blouse and the way it strained a little across her chest before returning to her face. The husky rattle of Kelsey's breathing seemed loud in the deafening silence of the cabin. Outside, more and more people were walking past, but inside it was eerily quiet – like a cocoon in the middle of a beehive.

'Did you want to wait for a bit until the number of passengers returning to their cabins lessens?'

The offer was a little stiff even if it did seem genuine enough, and it made perfect sense to wait. But still, she was too conscious of him as a man. It felt too... intimate.

'I think I've already interrupted your evening enough,' she said, waving her hand at his towel, her cheeks heating as she tried not to remember how aroused he'd been beneath that towel earlier.

'It's fine,' he assured. 'They shouldn't be too long and I can shower when you've gone. I'll just—' He indicated the wardrobe as he headed back her way. 'Put something else on.'

Kelsey nodded. Him *not* being in a towel would help.

He gestured to the chair at the small round corner coffee table. 'Take a seat. I'll be right back.'

Crossing to the chair, Kelsey sat as Ari disappeared into the bathroom and what sounded like a herd of people passed by outside. He was back in under a minute in track pants and a T-shirt.

'I'm having a whisky,' he said as he left the bathroom. 'Will you join me?'

Kelsey didn't think adding *drinking* with a passenger in his cabin to her list of transgressions was particularly wise, and whisky wasn't her favourite tipple, but they had to *do* something. 'Yes, thank you.'

He crossed to the open shelving above the in-built drawers and poured a shot of whisky into two glasses. He handed one to her then sat on the end of the bed. 'To the *Hellenic Spirit*, may she go well,' he said, raising his glass.

Kelsey raised hers. 'To the *Hellenic Spirit*.'

Despite the urge to slam the whole thing back, Kelsey sipped at the drink. So did Ari. 'Your headache is gone now?' she asked politely, fixing her gaze on his face and not the soft fall of his shirt against broad shoulders.

'Yes. I slept for a few hours before dinner and it was gone when I woke.'

'You looked good at dinner,' she agreed, and then her cheeks flushed as the full import of what she'd said dawned. 'I mean... you looked...' She groped around for a word that didn't involve the words sexy, hot or *fuckable*. 'Recovered.'

He gave her a small smile, like he knew exactly what she'd meant but that he'd found her slip of the tongue amusing. 'Thank you.'

'And how was your first evening meal on your first ever cruise?'

They passed ten minutes with inane chatter about the dining room and his trip to the casino like they hadn't kissed in this very room a handful of hours ago. In fact, between trying not to think about that and her ears straining for noises in the passageway, she barely took in a word he said.

The second it fell quiet outside, Kelsey stood, placing her barely touched shot of whisky down. 'I think it's all clear now.'

Manoeuvring around the table, she headed for the door, aware that Ari had also stood and was following close behind. Heat radiated from his body and her heart fluttered as it surrounded her, her legs turning to rubber. She reached for the doorknob the same time he did and their fingers connected.

A spark flared at his touch and it took all her willpower not to turn around and find out where that spark might lead because she'd already broken enough rules for one day.

She pulled at the doorknob. It didn't budge. 'Wait,' he said, his hold tightening around her hand. More voices became audible. They were further down but they'd no doubt see her if she tried to leave now.

Her heart beating like wings in her chest, she stood, straining her ears, praying for whoever it was to move on quickly as the heat from Ari's body both warmed and intoxicated in her in equal measure.

There was probably a foot between them but he might as well have been jammed against her. She could smell maple syrup and hear the unsteady timbre of his breathing.

Or maybe that was hers.

'I really am very sorry about the kiss,' he said, his voice low and husky, as the voices outside drew closer.

Kelsey shut her eyes. *God*, that kiss. It had been crazy. Sweet and simple. Innocent, almost. But it had lit her up. Just like she was lit up now.

She could only imagine how a *not* innocent kiss could be between them. How a full-on open-mouthed, head-rocking, lip-crushing kiss could be.

She wished she didn't want to know. But she did.

She really did.

3

Before she could stop herself, she turned and her pulse lurched at his nearness. Her legs shook and her hands shook and the sound of her heartbeat was so loud in her ears it drowned out the voices passing by in the corridor beyond the door.

Kelsey couldn't lift her eyes to him. Admitting her desire was bad enough – she couldn't be any bolder. Her gaze fixed on the uneven movement of his chest, the bob of his Adam's apple in his throat.

She should turn back. She should open the door. She should leave. The voices were hardly discernible now. But everything inside her burned to feel his mouth on hers again.

No matter how many rules she was breaking.

To pull him closer, not turn away. To throw caution to the wind like so many other staff members did and break a rule for once. Indulge herself a little in this private cocoon where nobody need know.

In seven years of employment, she'd never gone there. But maybe *just this once*, she could? In a year she'd be out of here, living in a small town with an increasingly dependent mother where there'd be zero opportunities to kiss a hot Greek dude.

Was it wrong to want just one wild moment to look back on and remember she'd had a little excitement in her life?

'Kelsey.'

It was a raw sound, a rumble delivered on a ragged exhalation. It could have meant go or stay or just *please*, but whatever it meant she'd felt it *everywhere*. Oozing like warm honey, caressing like cool silk, pulling like the tide.

The rough draw of his breath met the shallow husk of hers. Her knees wobbled. Her heart banged loud behind her ribs as she gathered the courage to meet his eyes. The hot spear of his gaze settled on her mouth and she was lost.

And hell... it was just a kiss.

She raised a trembling hand and slid it onto his shoulder.

Heat tingled in her fingers and danced up her arm as his muscles bunched beneath her palm. Then he took a step toward her, his body aligning with hers, pressing her into the door. He lifted his gaze, pierced her with a dark, unfathomable expression.

'This is madness,' he muttered.

'Yes,' she replied, but then he was lowering his head and Kelsey was powerless to do anything but meet him halfway.

This kiss was much more than the pressing together of two sets of lips. It was heat and electricity and fireworks. It was hard and deep. Wet and open. It was twisting tongues and clashing teeth. It was deep, rumbly groans and urgent nonsensical mutterings. It was a sudden storm, fork lightning and dumping rain.

Wreaking havoc.

There was no sense of control or propriety. No possible way to keep it in check. It was a wild frothing beast of a thing and Kelsey was a slave to it and his mouth.

Nobody had ever kissed her like this.

So... *needy*. Greedy, desperate kisses. Suffocating her with their urgency. Drawing from her as if she was oxygen and he was flame. Kisses that stole her breath but made her feel more fucking *alive* than she'd ever been.

Her pulse thrummed and blood flowed thick and fast, her ears ringing to the rhythm of her arousal. She was hot and wet and ready, her whole body humming. It was utterly insane.

She'd *never* wanted a man so absolutely, so damn fast. Hell, they hadn't even officially been introduced, and she *never* did something like this with a guy who hadn't introduced himself first.

Apart from earlier – but *that* kiss was *not* this kiss.

And she didn't need a crystal ball to know *this* wasn't just a kiss. That she couldn't stop at *just* a kiss. That she wanted more of him – all of him – and if she *was* crossing a line with Ari George, then she was going to do so in spectacular fashion.

He broke off, easing back slightly, their breathing hot and heavy. 'Are you sure?' he said, his gaze probing.

Kelsey liked that Ari also knew where this was heading. That this was more than just one kiss. She nodded – she'd never been surer in her life. It might be unwise, but there it was. She'd never indulged in anything so utterly reckless. She'd played by the rules and been a model employee but just this once, she was going to indulge in something for her – before she *settled* into a small town life.

'Are you?' she asked.

That he wanted her was obvious. She could feel the evidence of his arousal hard against her belly. But she swore she could see a hazy swirl of conflict in his eyes, like he wanted her but maybe he didn't *want* to want her.

If she'd been in her right mind she might have paid it more heed. Alas, she was not.

'Yes,' he muttered and kissed her again, his body pressing hard and urgent against hers, her head bumping the back of the door.

Kelsey's arms wrapped around his neck as she lost herself to his mouth, lost herself to the thrill and hum of her body, aware vaguely that her legs were moving and so were his but not really registering their progress until he stopped abruptly at the barrier of the bed.

He broke off and they stared at each other for a beat or two. The bed was right there behind him and she wanted him on it, she wanted to be *on him* on it. Placing her palm in the centre of his chest, she gave him a gentle shove, satisfied in a primal kind of way when he landed half reclined, his eyes dark, his mouth wet.

'Shirt,' she said, her voice an even huskier vibrato than normal.

He didn't say a word, just stripped his shirt off and tossed it aside.

'Those.' Her greedy gaze strayed to the large bulge straining against the front of his track pants as she pointed at them.

He didn't move for a beat or two but when he did, he stripped them down his legs in record time, taking his underwear down too, kicking them both away. And *oh-dear-good-fucking-Christ* he was art bought to life. A study in male beauty, laid out before her.

Naked and exposed for her viewing pleasure.

Pillows of muscle, hardness of bone. Planes and dips and ridges from the dark, stubbly stretch of his neck to the sturdiness of his clavicles. To the solid slabs of his quads and the prominence of his hip bones.

And that V, of course. That fascinating v of muscle slung between those two pelvic ridges, funnelling down to his groin and a part of his anatomy that widened Kelsey's eyes.

His cock was *all* the things.

Sprouting hard and rampant from the thatch of dark hair at his groin. Poised for action. Long. Thick. Taut. Perfectly veined. The crown engorged, flushed purple. The slipperiness between her legs kicked up a notch. Her clit throbbed.

A woman could become enthralled to that thing. Owned by it – whiling away her days screwing it, sucking it, writing poetry about it.

It was the kind of cock that inspired literature.

'Your turn.'

She dragged her gaze back to his face. Back to that mouth and those eyes watching her so intently. She was surprised her clothes hadn't just melted right off under his blatant eye-fucking.

Disrobing in front of a guy for the first time could be a little unnerving – even when there was an existing relationship. But the way he was looking at her, the way his dick surged against his belly and his chest rose and fell in a heavy, uneven rhythm, emboldened Kelsey.

In a flash, her shirt was over her head, her bra was unclasped and falling down her arms and she was wiggling out of her skirt at the same time she was kicking off her heels.

Kelsey knew she was perky and pretty. She'd been told that by guys ever since she'd lost her virginity at seventeen. But, at five two and a size twelve, she wasn't exactly supermodel skinny. Her stomach wasn't dead flat. There was some cellulite going on with her thighs.

He didn't seem to care.

'*Theé*,' he muttered, deep and ragged as his gaze zeroed in on her breasts like *they* were all the things.

She moved then, taking two steps and climbing on the bed, climbing on him, straddling his hips, settling the slickness between her legs over the hardness between his. His hands slid to her thighs and she rubbed against his dick, eliciting a groan that filled the charged air with a cocktail of pheromones.

He vaulted up then, an arm snaking around her waist, pulling her in tight and close as his mouth claimed first one nipple then the other. Kelsey's gasp soon turned to a moan, her arms circling his head as his mouth set up a lick, swirl, suck pattern that had stars bursting behind her eyelids.

If this had been his job, she'd have awarded him employee of the month.

But it still wasn't enough. A wild kind of hunger roared in her blood, beating like a drum at her pulse points and rushing like Niagara Falls through her ears. Kelsey needed more. She needed *all* of him.

She ground the heavy, aching lips of her sex along the hard ridge of his shaft. It was so damn good it sucked her breath away and he groaned against her nipple, bucking his hips to meet the reckless demands of her body.

His hand slid between them and Kelsey gasped as his finger found the tight knot of nerves and stroked it over and over as he licked his way up her neck. *Oh man!* It'd been a long time between orgasms and she was going to come embarrassingly quickly if he kept that up.

'*Fuuuck*,' she whispered, squeezing her eyes shut as the cabin seemed to tilt.

She whimpered as his fingers slid lower and his mouth worked higher. His tongue was hot and wet at her earlobe, somehow opening up a sensory pathway straight to her clit, stimulating it with every flick of his tongue. Kelsey moaned and ground against him again as Ari guided his cock, thick and ready, to her entrance.

Thankfully it was enough to rouse her from the stupor drugging her sensibilities. 'No, wait... Stop.' She was breathing hard as she grabbed hold of his wrist. 'Condom.'

He stared blankly for a beat or two then pressed his forehead between her breasts. '*Christe...*' His breathing was laboured as he lifted his head, his gaze finding hers. 'I don't have a condom.'

Kelsey gave a half laugh. 'Yes, you do. You have two in your wallet.'

He blinked. 'I... do?'

She nodded. 'I saw them there.'

'It must have been Theo,' he said, almost to himself. 'My brother.'

'Does it matter?' she asked, conscious of his cock still thick and hard between her legs.

'Hell no.'

He kissed her again – brief and cataclysmic – before they disengaged, half crawling, half wriggling up the bed in a tangle of arms and legs and sheets. Kelsey didn't notice the crisp freshness of the linen or the fat comfort of the pillows, just Ari rolling on his side, grabbing his wallet, rifling through it and pulling out a foil packet.

Kelsey watched, her entire body flushed with arousal and anticipation as he tore it open and sheathed his cock. Then he was reaching for her, rolling on top of her, his hips aligning with hers, his cock dragging through the slick furrow of her sex, spiking her pulse and hitching her breath. He stared at her intently as he slowly ground his cock against her aching core, shooting a hot streak of lust up her spine.

Kelsey clutched his shoulders and arched into him, locking her legs around the backs of his thighs. He ground again, taking full advantage of their horizontal position.

'Yes,' she whispered into his neck as the thick crown notched full against her entrance. 'There, right there.'

He thrust, groaning something deep and guttural and definitely not English into her ear as he slid into her, thick and solid and good.

So. Damn. Good.

Kelsey cried out, sliding her hands down his back to grasp his clenched ass cheeks, holding him there. They both stilled for a moment, their breathing thick and loud.

Kelsey was the first to recover. 'More,' she whispered.

He raised his head, their gazes locking, and Kelsey's breath caught at the undiluted lust she saw in Ari's eyes, at the tightly leashed power. His body was trembling and she knew he was holding himself in check.

'All of it,' she muttered before raising her head off the bed and kissing him.

He met her halfway, swooping down to claim her mouth, to plunder it with his tongue, to dominate it, to own it with every twist of his head. Kelsey's world turned molten, her veins lava tubes coursing through her body as she clung to him, taking and giving with equal ferocity.

His hips moved too. Slow and steady, but *fuck that*. She didn't want slow and steady. She wanted pure uninhibited man. She wanted him to fuck her the way he was kissing her – deep and dirty. She was committing an act that was, in essence, a sackable offence.

For damn sure, it had better blow her freaking mind.

She shifted, arched, squirmed, opened her hips a little further and cried out when he slid in higher and harder on a low, guttural groan. And it was like the chains that were leashing him suddenly broke, the shackles falling away, and he plundered her pussy like he was plundering her mouth – relentlessly.

His hips were a piston, rocking her closer and closer. Rocking *him* closer and closer. His ass tightening, his back bowing, his mouth tearing from hers, his lips pressing behind her ear as he groaned and panted and called out to God.

'*Theé, mou.*'

And then he slipped his hands between them, his fingers deftly finding her hair-trigger state, causing Kelsey to also call out to God.

In a much less poetic way.

'Jesus... fuck! *Christ!* I'm coming.'

And she was. One stroke of his finger – two – and a violent flare of sensation burst out from the taut bundle of nerves, strangling her breath in her throat. Her body bucked and bowed, subsumed by the tremors of her release, her legs locking tight around his waist as her pussy clamped tight around his cock.

He came too, gasping his release right into her ear with another string of words in his mother tongue that somehow managed to sound like ancient Greek literature and pornography all at once. They spun her higher and faster, pushing her into another realm, a dizzying aphrodisiac as he chased her into the thick fugue of bliss.

* * *

Kelsey lost all touch with time and space for what seemed like hours but what was, in actuality, only a few minutes. When she came back to herself, Ari was easing himself off, rolling onto his back.

Neither said anything for long moments as he removed the condom and disposed of it in the bin. Kelsey was just content to lie in the bliss. Not psychoanalyse what had just happened. Not worry about the potential for career and therefore financial disaster.

Frankly, it didn't *feel* like a disaster. There was no sense of doom lying here next to him, just the feeling that it'd been worth the risk.

And surely a one-off could be contained?

'My name is Ari George,' he said suddenly, his voice a low rasp into the quiet of the room.

Kelsey lifted her head, their eyes meeting. A slight smile played on his mouth as if he was as bemused as her by what had just occurred. 'Kelsey Armitage.'

And they both laughed.

* * *

Ari stared at the ceiling as Kelsey, curled into his side, drew patterns on his chest. He should be chilled out considering the orgasm he'd just experienced, but there was a wildly emotional tug-of-war going on inside his chest right now.

He felt... good. *Alive.*

Not dead and cold and desolate like he had for so long. But warm and breathing, his pulse flowing through his temples and thumping in his groin. There was a lightness in his chest he'd forgotten used to be normal.

And that was utterly terrifying.

What the fuck? How could three years of darkness just suddenly break into light? He didn't know how to *exist* in the light any more. He *liked* the dark.

He knew his way around there.

He didn't know who this person was who *smiled* at cocktail umbrellas and kissed a woman he barely knew – *fucked* a woman he barely knew.

Why didn't he feel terrible? And disloyal. And disrespectful. To Talia. To her memory. Why hadn't he thought about her even once? When had he *stopped* thinking about her every second of the day?

Why did he feel *good*?

The only thing that made any sense of it was what his therapist had been fond of repeating. About grief not having a smooth trajectory. That there'd be ups and downs and backward slips, and Ari clung to the thought that this was some weird kind of *up*. That wouldn't last.

Some kind of aberration before he slid back into the familiar folds of darkness. That *had* to be it.

'Is Ari your proper name?'

The enquiry yanked him out of his psychoanalysis like a tug to his hair. Her enquiry was soft and low, not accusatory or suspicious, but Ari was already tense enough without Kelsey digging into his background.

'I mean, is it just Ari, or is it short for something?'

Relief, cool and fresh, flowed through Ari's body – the enquiry had been innocent. Still... he'd just had sex with a woman whilst pretending to be someone else. Sex with a woman who wasn't Talia.

Guilt layered on top of guilt.

'It's short for Aristotle.'

'So, no pressure then,' she said and laughed.

Despite his inner turmoil, Ari laughed too. What was it about Kelsey that put him so damn at ease? 'I don't think my parents thought I'd follow in the great philosopher's footsteps or anything. It's just a common Greek name.'

'You sound very English for a Greek guy. Were you born there?'

'No. I was born in Athens.' Being dragged out of his head into normal, everyday conversation was helping with the tight knots of tension in Ari's muscles. It felt good to be able to tell some truths right now. And Theo always insisted the best way to execute a lie was to stick to the truth as much as possible. 'But I lived in the UK for a long time.'

'Oh? Whereabouts?'

'London.'

Ari waited for the familiar stab of pain, the feeling of loss that came every time he thought about his decade in London. But it didn't. There was just an odd kind of ache that felt like something akin to nostalgia.

And that was terrifying too. The stab was always wrenching but it was familiar. The kind of pain that kept his love and his memories alive.

The knots tightened again.

'London is amazing,' she said, her voice rich with affection. 'Did you work there?'

'Yes. For ten years.'

She rolled up onto her elbow and looked down at him, her hair falling around her face and brushing her shoulders, her cupid's bow pursing a little. She was so lovely Ari's heart skipped a beat. 'And what do you do, Aristotle George?'

'I'm an accountant.'

That was the truth. He *was* an accountant. He just happened to be the *chief* accountant of a billion-dollar business.

'Really?' She raised an eyebrow, clearly surprised. 'And here I thought all accountants were boring guys with glasses who were wizards with numbers and tax law, not' – she stroked her index finger along his bottom lip – 'making women come.'

For a moment, Ari let her compliment go to his head. He'd forgotten how good it felt to be flattered by a woman. 'You should never judge a book by its cover.'

'Oh, trust me. I'm never going to look at another accountant the same *ever* again.'

The thought of Kelsey looking at other accountants, looking at other men for that matter, was disconcerting. Which was confusing as fuck. Why should he care who she looked at?

'Happy to be addressing stereotypes,' he said, to cover his confusion.

She laughed and Ari's lungs felt too big for his chest as she laid her head on his shoulder again and went back to swirling patterns against his skin.

Her fingers stopped after a minute and he started to wonder if she was asleep. A trickle of adrenaline kicked in, stirring uneasily through his gut. This was all too much. Too fast. He hadn't *slept* with a woman since Talia, and that would be plain... weird, right?

Spending all night in bed with someone other than his wife?

But he needn't have worried; Kelsey didn't linger for long, rolling into a sitting position a minute later, her feet landing on the floor. 'I have to go.'

Ari didn't stop her. He didn't protest. He didn't ask her to stay. Even though, perversely, he didn't want her to go.

She padded to the end of the bed and picked up her clothes, suddenly businesslike as she looked at him and said, 'You know we can't do this again, right?'

Ari nodded, the adrenaline in his system ebbing. Yes. *Fuck yes*. It had been a crazy kind of interlude, a moment of weakness, a reaction to three long dark years of heartache and sorrow.

Or something. He didn't know exactly.

He'd figure out how it fit into the jigsaw of his grief – because what other explanation was there? – later, after the cruise was over.

For now, it was done.

'Yeah. I know.'

She disappeared into the bathroom but kept the door open. 'Just to clarify,' she said, her voice floating out to him, 'that means no flirting with me in the dining room or trying to monopolise my time at the bar, or asking other staff about me.'

'I know.' Ari didn't need any clarification. He wanted exactly the same thing.

'I don't want anyone guessing something happened between us.'

'They won't.'

His response must have been a touch too flippant for her because she stepped out of the bathroom looking at him like he didn't fully appreciate the stakes. She was in her skirt and bra, which was seriously hot and made him realise his head and his body were in two different places.

The thought was slightly mollifying. Physical attraction was easier to dismiss.

'I'm not kidding around.' Her gaze nailed him to the bed as she stuck her hands into her blouse and pulled it over her head. 'I could lose my job.'

Ari fixed her with a steady gaze as her head reappeared from the fabric. 'I *don't* kiss and tell.'

What had happened in this room with Kelsey would stay in this room. And hopefully not accompany him all around the goddamn ship. Replaying on an endless loop in his brain.

'Good.' She nodded as she smoothed her shirt at the waist. 'But to clarify even further, a one-and-done thing includes not getting in touch after the cruise as well. No exchanging emails. No sliding into my Instagram DMs.'

If Ari had been in a different emotional place he might have been insulted by how completely Kelsey wanted to sever their connection. But the implications of what they'd done weighed on him too, even if it was for totally different reasons. 'Not on any social media.'

Most people usually looked at him strangely when he said that, but Kelsey didn't bat an eyelid; she just kept right on going. 'I know we'll probably run into each other around the ship from time to time – that's unavoidable. But the second this ship docks in Venice, it's goodbye forever.'

The thought of never seeing Kelsey again should have cheered him, and Ari nodded and said, 'Absolutely,' but there was an unexpected hitch right in the centre of his chest which was utter madness.

Kelsey was a... one night stand. It was preposterous to *feel* anything.

'Okay then.' She stepped into her shoes, her height rising by two inches. 'I guess I'll be seeing you around.'

Ari nodded. '*Kalinita,* Kelsey.'

She didn't return his goodnight; she just turned and strode to the door, paused briefly to listen for noise in the passageway, then opened it and slipped out.

The door clicked shut two seconds later. Ari couldn't decide if he was relieved or bereft...

4

At eleven thirty the next morning, Kelsey was out the back of the pool deck bar cutting up fruit during a lull in customers, trying not to think about last night. She'd managed to slice three oranges when her partner for the shift, Rasheesh – one of the beverage managers who often did a shift to keep his skills up – called out, 'Service, please.'

Washing her hands quickly under the tap, she dried and wiped them before heading around front to find Rasheesh talking to a group of people as he made a theatrical show of mixing a cocktail. And the man she'd been daydreaming about sitting at the end of the bar.

Her step faltered as their gazes locked. Ari's presence was like a sudden zap of static electricity, and not just because he looked devastating in a casual T-shirt fitted snug across his chest and biceps. Or the fact he hadn't shaved, taking the stubble firmly into whisker territory. But because he said he wasn't going to do this – monopolise her attention when she was working.

It made her super conscious of her indiscretion, although, to be fair to him, Ari seemed as surprised by her presence. It wasn't like the man was privy to her work schedule.

'Can you serve the gentleman at the end?' Rasheesh prompted as Kelsey dithered for a moment.

She nodded. There was little else she could do with the cocktail crowd at the bar and Rasheesh frowning at her uncharacteristic inaction.

'Good morning, sir,' she said, approaching him with her most polite smile in situ. 'What can I get you?' She winced internally at how formal she sounded.

'Whisky, please. Neat.' Ari was equally as formal.

Kelsey poured the drink then put it down on a white bar napkin in front of him. Ari glanced at Rasheesh then back at her saying, 'Sorry,' as he lifted the drink, the glass hiding his lips. 'I didn't know you'd be here.'

She gave a brief nod. Unfortunately, whether it was deliberate or accidental, she couldn't ignore him, especially not in front of one of the bosses. It was her job to be polite, to 'make idle chit chat' with the customer; hell, even flirt a little if it meant a nice tip and a passenger deciding to upgrade to a more expensive alcohol package.

Which Kelsey would have been more than happy to try with *any other passenger*. But with Ari, she was determined to keep this conversation professional – no matter how hot he looked this morning.

'You're not going to check out Naples today, sir?' she enquired, projecting her voice a little for the benefit of Rasheesh.

They'd docked early this morning and 90 per cent of the passengers had disembarked to spend a day in one of Italy's most popular tourist destinations.

He shook his head. 'I don't really get what the fuss is about Naples.'

Kelsey agreed wholeheartedly, but publicly dissing one of their ports was frowned upon. 'You've been before?'

He nodded. 'Several times.'

'You could take a tour to Pompeii?' she said, her tone firmly suggestive. Him being off the ship most days would be better for avoidance purposes.

A tight smile crossed his lips and she knew damn well he'd received her message loud and clear. 'I'm probably going to stay on the ship most days.'

Kelsey blinked, her brain grappling with the revelation. Ari had confessed to being a cruise virgin, so surely he'd want to disembark at every stop and see all there was to see?

'I'd have thought you'd want to explore more given this is your first cruise?'

He shrugged. 'I'm only planning on getting off at Mykonos.'

Kelsey's brows rose. 'Not Athens? Or Santorini?' They were the two most popular stops on the cruise.

'No.' He said it in a clipped kind of way that sounded very Greek. 'I know them both well and I prefer Mykonos.'

It struck Kelsey that Ari might have been better off taking a cruise to the Caribbean rather than an area with which he was so familiar. But maybe he hadn't wanted to go too far afield.

'I love the beaches and sitting in all the little bars on the water's edge,' he continued. 'I love its laid-back vibe.'

She nodded, his words disarming her resolve to stay polite but aloof. 'I love Mykonos too.' She loved being closer to the water. Her favourite thing to do was to sit in one of those bars and stare at the windmills.

'A woman of taste.'

His dark gaze held hers briefly before he downed his drink in one swallow, as he had yesterday. She watched the shift of muscles in his throat and the fascinating coverage of his whiskers.

Damn it all – why couldn't the man just leave the ship every day like a *normal* passenger?

Tapping the rim, he said, 'Another.'

Acutely aware she was staring and that he knew she was staring, Kelsey poured the drink. 'What are your plans for on board then, sir?'

Her voice wobbled a little at calling him *sir*. It sounded kinda dirty in public given what had happened in private and it was the last thing Kelsey needed on her mind.

'Karaoke? Trivia?' Kelsey didn't care, as long as it was far away from her. 'There's a martini appreciation class going on in the main bar? Or maybe,' she said with saccharine sweetness, annoyed that he was making her feel hot and bothered just from his very presence, 'some bingo?'

The man looked like he played blackjack, not bingo, but he was a mass of contradictions. Here he was, a handsome – hell, *really fucking hot* – professional guy, travelling *alone* on a cruise ship. From the T-shirt he was wearing to the suit she'd seen him in last night, to that damn room towel, he oozed sex appeal.

Everything from the way he wore his clothes to the way he held himself screamed style and class. He looked like the kind of guy who could have a Kardashian on his arm and splash out on a suite – with a balcony.

So which Ari George was the real one? T-shirt or suit? Bingo or blackjack? Inside cabin or whisky in the morning?

'I'm going to the spa for a massage.'

Kelsey swallowed as thoughts of him naked and supine on a massage table, glistening with oil, rose in her mind. Her friend, Sachiko, was working in the spa today and Kelsey was suddenly jealous.

'The spa services are top rate.'

Somehow, she managed to keep her voice calm and her breathing even despite the pictures multiplying in her brain. Images of her hands on him, gliding all over his slick, supple muscles, her hands working and kneading, watching as his cock hardened beneath his towel and her fingers slid beneath...

He drained his glass and placed it down on the bar with a thunk, snapping Kelsey out of her daydream. 'Thank you for the drink.' He slid off the stool, pulled his wallet out and thrust a twenty-euro note in her direction.

Kelsey stared at the money as if it was a tarantula. It was obviously a tip but it felt... *icky* to take his money, and she was pissed off he'd even offered. In fact, she was about to refuse but Rasheesh approached and she quickly accepted it because it would appear odd not to and she didn't need the attention.

'Thank you, sir,' she said, taking the money, but he was already walking away, every inch the blackjack player.

* * *

Kelsey was still ticked about the tip an hour later as she headed to her lunch break. In fact, she was probably *more* annoyed thanks to the continuing barrage of unhelpful images keeping her company since Ari had departed. She didn't know how it was possible to be insulted and turned on all at once but that was absolutely her current state of being.

So she totally acted on impulse when she spotted Ari just ahead as she made her way to the mess. Totally reacted to the proximity of the staff-only room used to house linen and cleaning equipment.

Casting a quick glance around them to establish they were alone in the passageway, she said, 'Pardon me, sir.' She raised her voice a little to get his attention, her pulse fluttering madly at her daring.

He stopped, turned at her voice, frowned when his eyes met hers. 'Could I have a word with you, please?'

He glanced at the door as Kelsey yanked it open and a flare of heat lit the darkness of his gaze. Her breath hitched at the raw naked need she saw there, and for a moment the knowledge that this was a *very bad idea* pulsed openly between them and she thought he might refuse.

He did not.

Brushing past her, he entered and Kelsey followed him inside. Checking no one had seen them, she eased the door gently shut. They had a tendency to bang if allowed to close without assistance. Passengers didn't like it and she sure as hell didn't want to advertise their location.

The light was significantly reduced with the door shut, but Kelsey could feel the charge in the air from Ari's presence as she slowly turned. There was probably only a few feet separating them and he was backed against a set of shelves that held folded sheets. His whole frame was taut as a bow as he eyed her warily, clearly trying to keep as much distance between them as possible.

For which Kelsey was grateful.

But with her eyes adjusting to the low light, Kelsey couldn't help but notice the way he filled out his shirt or the fascinating bulge behind the zipper of his fly. It appeared he was as turned on by this clandestine meeting as she was.

Lordy, she wished she'd never discovered how good he was with that thing.

His hands curled and uncurled convulsively by his side. '*Christe, dósei mou éna diáleimma Kelsey.*'

Kelsey had no idea what he'd said but it was clearly based in frustration. His voice was gravel, his eyes hooded as she dragged her gaze from his crotch to his face.

'Talk, Kelsey,' he said, his voice deep and low. 'I'm trying really hard here but if you keep looking at me like that... I can't guarantee what might happen next.'

Kelsey was grateful for the solid presence of the door close behind her at his dirty rumble. Her body flamed, threatening to set everything, including her common sense, on fire. Clearing her throat, she dragged her brain back from the tug of a hundred different sex-in-confined-spaces scenarios.

But then his hands furled and unfurled by his sides again and her gaze dropped to follow the movement, and before she knew it her eyes were drawn once more to that bulge. Ari made some kind of guttural noise in the back of his throat, moving suddenly in her direction, backing her up until her ass hit the door.

Kelsey's heart pounded and her breath clogged thick as fog in the back of her throat as he placed the flats of his forearms either side of her head, pressed his body into hers and kissed her with such potent hunger and greed the back of her head *thunked* against the door.

'God,' he said on a groan. 'I can't stop thinking about you.' His mouth left hers and blazed a trail of kisses down her neck, his hands sliding low, settling on her ass and squeezing, melting the muscles in her pelvic floor.

Kelsey had been thinking of little else as well, her mind vacillating between heated memories of last night and annoyance over the tip. But it was hard to think of anything other than succumbing to the promise of his lips, the erotic scrape of his whiskers and the squeeze of his hands.

Liquid heat pooled between her hips and her legs felt as if they were made of marshmallow, but there were still a few brain cells functioning and she grabbed hold of them before things devolved any further. She sucked in a deep hard breath and reached for her earlier annoyance.

'Stop.' She pressed a hand to his chest, trying to give herself space to breathe. To think. 'We need to talk.'

He gave a deep strangled groan, burying his forehead into the crook of her neck as his hands stopped their dizzying rhythm. His harsh, ragged pants puffed hot air against her collarbone.

Ari lifted his head, a frustrated kind of torment haunting his dark eyes as their gazes met. But he eased his hands from her ass and took two paces backwards until he bumped up against the shelves again.

If possible, with his mouth wet from their kisses, he looked hotter, and Kelsey gripped the door handle behind her for support.

'I really didn't know you were at that bar. I couldn't see you when I arrived or I wouldn't have sat down.'

'I know.' Kelsey waved his explanation away. She had bigger fish to fry.

He frowned. 'Okay, so... why are we here?' He stared at her with an intensity she was getting used to, his gaze roving over her like she was a particularly interesting spreadsheet.

Kelsey forced herself to concentrate, to answer his question. 'Don't tip me.' She winced at how blunt and awkward it sounded, hurrying to qualify. 'If our paths happen to cross in a work capacity, don't tip me.'

'But...' His frown deepened. 'Why wouldn't I tip you for good service? I would do it for anyone.'

Kelsey could see his point but it didn't matter. 'Don't do it for me.'

His frown deepened. 'Don't tips make up a significant portion of your wage? Should you be knocking them back?'

She rolled her eyes. 'I won't miss the odd tip from one person. It makes me feel uncomfortable, Ari. Like you're using a tip as a proxy for payment of... other services.'

His stance suddenly got very erect. 'That was *not* what I was doing.'

His quick, hot denial was unnecessary but welcome. 'I know, I know.' Kelsey held her hands up in a placatory manner. 'It's just that some passengers think tips buy them special privileges.'

In her time on cruise ships she'd been blatantly groped, *accidentally* brushed up against, propositioned, and the butt of plenty of male passenger sleazy innuendo.

He straightened even further. '*What?* Does the cruise line know about this?'

'Of course.'

'And they just...' He looked utterly aghast. 'Let it happen? Let their staff be sexually harassed like that?'

Kelsey shrugged. 'Some ships are better at it than others so you mostly learn how to deal with that class of passenger yourself.'

'And what about this ship?'

Kelsey shook her head dismissively. 'They're a bit hit and miss but... that's not my point.' She didn't want to get sidetracked. 'Just don't, okay? That's all I'm asking.'

He stared at her for long seconds, his mouth in a straight hard line, the angle of his jaw blanching white beneath the dark growth of his whiskers. Then he dragged in a deep breath and the taut line of his shoulders relaxed. 'Of course,' he said with a nod. 'Whatever you want.'

Oh *dear lord* no. What she wanted right now was unspeakable.

Kelsey swallowed. 'Thank you. I appreciate it.' And now they needed to get the hell out of this tiny, *tiny* room. 'I'm going to check the corridor is all clear,' she said, taking charge. 'And then I'm going to leave. You wait for a minute, check it's still all clear then leave too.'

He quirked an eyebrow. 'Should we synchronise our watches?'

She shot him a quelling look, which he waved away. 'Go.' His gaze dropped to her mouth. Dropped lower to the snug fit of her polo shirt before returning to her face. 'Now.'

Kelsey turned, opened the door and stepped outside, her legs wobbly, her heart racing.

* * *

Ari was distracted during dinner that night. Jean Paul, the maître d' – a fit-looking man in his fifties with silver hair and plenty of swagger – had suggested the previous evening that Ari might like to try a different table every night rather than sticking to the same one. To meet *all* the ladies, he had said with a hearty slap on the back.

Ari wasn't keen on the smoothness of the maître d' but he was clearly popular with the female passengers and it *was* sensible advice to get to meet as many people as possible. And that was, after all, what he was here for – to meet fellow passengers, garner their experiences, find out about their gripes.

Get to the bottom of the problems with the *Hellenic Spirit*.

It was a shame he was being constantly distracted by Kelsey. She was at the opposite end of the restaurant to him, but the bob and swish of her blonde ponytail was like a magnet in his peripheral vision, a constant reminder of their tête-à-tête earlier. Of how he'd tried *so damn hard* not to put his hands on her in that godforsaken *cupboard,* of how she'd looked at him with heat and hunger and destroyed all his resolve.

He didn't want to feel this way, *damn it.*

'Can you pass the bread please?'

Ari dragged himself out of his head and smiled at the woman beside him. She was an American, diamonds glittering on her fingers and at her throat. Her hair was elegantly greying and she had a tightness to her face that did not match her neck or hands. Her husband was wearing a ten thousand-dollar suit and, if Ari was not very much mistaken, had also had some work done around his eyes. He was in crypto apparently.

There were three other couples around the table. Two of them were travelling with Mr and Mrs Bitcoin and were obviously as wealthy, talking about the time they all stayed in Monte Carlo. The seat beside him was vacant, but on the opposite side of the table were a couple from Lancashire, celebrating their fortieth wedding anniversary.

He'd been a factory worker all of his life, and his wife worked as a care assistant in a nursing home. They were dressed well but it was clear they were not in the same socio-economic class as the other couples at the table. Not that it seemed to matter to anyone. The Americans were including the English couple and himself in their conversations and were interested in life in the UK and Athens.

The only person that seemed to have trouble with the wealth disparity between the passengers was the waiter allocated to their table. His name was Sameel, he looked about twenty-five and he was new to cruising. The *Hellenic Spirit* was his first vessel and this cruise was his first after completing his training a few weeks ago.

And so far, he wasn't doing so great.

Whilst he wasn't exactly rude to the English couple or Ari, he was far more attentive to the Americans. He fussed over them to the point of obsequiousness and turned himself inside out to correct the error when one of their steaks arrived medium rather than rare. Meanwhile, the gentleman from Lancashire had asked twice for some mustard and it still hadn't arrived.

Ari made a mental note and filed it away for later as, once again, his peripheral vision snagged on the swish and bob of Kelsey's ponytail. He surrendered to the urge to watch her for a moment or two, drawn to her in a way he didn't understand. She was in silhouette, framed by the large round porthole to her rear, and the golden rays of the sun setting over the Mediterranean temporarily set her aflame.

His breath caught at the sight. It felt like a metaphor for her impact on his life and it was hard to believe he'd met her for the first time only yesterday.

How was that even possible?

Sameel took his plate away, regaining Ari's attention, and his eyes took a tour of the restaurant as the waiter busied himself with clearing the table. It was a huge two-floor behemoth with a sweeping circular staircase in the middle leading to the upper floor. An expensive chandelier crafted in Murano hung above the staircase.

Modern décor gave the surroundings an elegant but charming feel, supported by the low orchestral music playing through the state-of-the-art sound system. Large scattered urns of greenery and fresh flowers were the perfect foil to the deep blue of the sea, providing a shifting canvas through the multiple portholes.

On one side of the restaurant, the colour and chaos of Naples grew smaller, and on the other, the horizon lay steady and unwavering.

Ari's attention was snagged by Crypto Dude discreetly slipping some euros into Sameel's hand. Sameel took it just as discreetly, aside from the smile on his face as big as the room.

Ari didn't begrudge him the tip. He knew, as he had told Kelsey earlier, that tips helped bolster what could be a very basic wage for a junior staff member.

But they shouldn't be used to discriminate against passengers. All passengers were to be treated as equals – that was the Ōceanós way.

He'd actually noticed similar staff behaviour at a couple of bars around the ship as well. Preferential service, going that extra mile for wealthier passengers. And, if he'd noticed, maybe the passengers were noticing as well? Nobody wanted to spend thousands of dollars of their hard-earned money and be made to feel like a second-class citizen.

It was troubling behaviour. Maybe even a pattern? All a ship needed was a few bad eggs to influence the staff culture. Obviously not all staff engaged in discriminating behaviour, but there shouldn't be *any*.

The captain arrived at the table. The American men went to stand but the captain waved them back into their seats as Sameel performed the introductions. He got the English woman's name wrong but nailed the names of the wealthy at the table and spent an inordinate amount of time singing their praises.

Ari was vaguely acquainted with Captain Russo. They had met a long time ago at an Ōceanós event, but he showed no recognition now of the Callisthenes family *recluse*.

A badge Ari wore with pride.

After a lifetime of flashbulbs and cameras following him everywhere, Ari had been well and truly ready to escape them when he'd moved to London to study, and it had been his salvation. Then he'd met Talia and, despite her own pedigree, they'd been content to live in complete anonymity amidst London's thriving boroughs, even declining the obscene amounts of money offered for the pictorial rights to their very private wedding.

It was no surprise the captain didn't recognise him. That was the whole point of Ari doing this investigation.

Captain Russo was excellent at his job. He'd been with Ōceanós for a dozen years captaining various ships and his qualifications were impeccable. Unfortunately, listening to him in person wasn't a particularly thrilling experience. He obviously suffered a little too much under the weight of his own importance.

Ari's grandfather always said that doctors and lawyers had nothing on the arrogance of a ship's captain, and now Ari knew exactly what the old man meant.

Russo was no Captain Stubbing, that was for sure.

He was also, like Sameel, a little more effusive with the wealthier clientele, which was disappointing. Maybe this preferential treatment thing *was* systemic? Attitude always came from the top down and Ari made a mental note to cross-check the ship's performance with Russo's tenure at the helm.

With his allotted five minutes up, the captain made his apologies and moved on, but not without first shaking the hands of the three American men at the table, sparing only a brief touch to his brim for Ari and the Lancashire factory worker.

Ari's misgivings about the ship's culture weighed heavily on him as the captain moved to the next table. He wasn't liking what he was seeing. He wasn't liking it one little bit.

5

It was still bugging Ari the next morning. Or rather the first thing he'd thought about when he'd woken this morning had been Kelsey, and that was putting him in the kind of mood where everything bugged him.

He'd known her for *two* days. How was it even possible that she was the first face he saw when he opened his eyes? That position had always belonged to Talia and Ari had panicked as he'd struggled for a beat or two to instantly recall her face.

She came – of course she came – but those confused seconds had been disorientating. And worrying. And guilt had once again taken hold. What if one day he just simply couldn't recall his dead wife's face any more?

Those thoughts had driven him out of the cabin. Out of the place where Kelsey's face and her laughter and her moans waited for him in every corner.

Where they *beckoned*.

Pushing those thoughts aside, he stepped into the passageway with his day planned out in his mind. First stop was the breakfast buffet and then he was going to do the rounds of the different restaurants, lounges and bars.

Minus the pool deck bar, of course. And not because of Kelsey but because he'd already checked it out a couple of times now and had made his notes on it already. He'd been pleased with how it was being run – his missing twenty euros notwithstanding.

Ari reached the mid-ship lift foyer and decided to eschew the elevator for the wide staircase connecting all the decks. Taking the steps two at a time to level fourteen, his heart was pumping a little harder by the time he pushed open the heavy door and stepped out onto the top deck.

A light breeze ruffled though his hair and he sucked in the sweet fresh air as he stopped at the railing admiring the endless stretch of sapphire water that was the Med. She was an undeniable beauty, the kind of blue that was hard to explain, and this sea was in his bones as surely as the Acropolis and Ouzo.

He pulled himself away – reluctantly – a few minutes later, following a group of people into the buffet. His mouth watered at the aromas wafting from the massive restaurant to the aft of the ship and his stomach growled in unison. He was absolutely ravenous.

Ari entered the restaurant and found his own seat, which was the way of buffet-style dining. The only problem with that was there was no staff member on the door with a pump container full of hand sanitiser offering it to passengers as was the practice in all the other dining areas of the ship.

Sure, there was a table at the entrance with a pump and a sign urging people to use it, but that wasn't good enough as far as Ari – and the ship protocols – were concerned. Mandatory offering of hand sanitiser was one of the measures that had been instituted two years ago across all the ships in the fleet to reduce the incidence of gastroenteritis.

Studies had shown people were more likely to use the sanitiser if it was presented to them as a natural part of the seating process.

Another measure they'd actioned to stem outbreaks had been switching to a no self-serve buffet. It was protocol now for staff members to serve the requested food to passengers. This reduced the risk of cross contamination by people whose diligence with hand washing – particularly after toileting – was often subpar.

The buffet restaurant failed miserably in this department, which was concerning considering the weight of evidence pointing to cruise ships' buffets being the major source for gastro outbreaks. Some staff members were good, politely insisting on serving the passengers, but most turned a blind eye to those helping themselves.

Ari made mental notes as he took everything in. It was going to be a long day, he could tell.

* * *

By three in the afternoon he was sitting at the piano bar on deck four, which was tucked away beside the Adelphi Theatre. There was him and a couple sitting in a booth near the piano, their heads close together as they listened to a middle-aged guy tickle the ivories. The atmosphere was more intimate in this establishment with a lot of wood and dark furniture but, thanks to light spilling in from the three large portholes behind the bar, it was saved from looking too much like a private men's club.

The bulk of the day trippers hadn't yet returned from shore and Ari was enjoying the lack of people as well as one of the fine cognacs on the menu. It was the perfect spot to make notes for his report, check in with Theo and deal with any urgent business that required his attention.

Also to think. Not about Kelsey – absolutely *not* about Kelsey. But to ponder things like the disparity in staff treatment between passengers of differing socio-economic backgrounds, which was still a source of irritation.

They couldn't afford to have that kind of class system on their ships. They had exclusive cruises catering solely to very wealthy clientele, but this was an everyman kind of cruise and reputation was paramount. It was imperative that all passengers were treated with equal respect.

'A penny for them, sir.'

Ari pulled his gaze away from the left-hand porthole, startled at the familiar voice. *Kelsey*. So much for avoiding her. It appeared, whether he wanted to think about her or not, the universe was just going to keep shoving her under his nose. This morning he'd been overwhelmed with how quickly she'd taken up his headspace. This afternoon he was struck by the wave of pleasure he felt at her *we-really-should-stop-meeting-like-this* smile.

She was in the formal uniform she usually wore in the dining room.

The one she'd stripped out of in his room. Ari's lungs felt too big for his chest as he batted down that particularly errant thought.

Concentrate, Aristotle.

'I'm sorry,' he said, his voice low as he glanced over his shoulder at the couple who were paying them absolutely zero attention. 'I thought you'd be working on the pool deck.'

She shrugged. 'I'm just covering for the next hour or so.'

He put his phone in his pocket and slid his feet off the footrest of the barstool to the ground. 'I'll go.'

'No. Stay.' She waved him back into his seat with a sigh. 'You look comfortable and it's hardly crowded in here.'

Ari looked around again. 'Why do you think I'm here?'

She gave him a grudging smile. 'You're not much of a people person, are you?' she said as she picked up his glass. 'Can I get you another?'

'Yes. Thank you. Cognac.'

He watched as she got him a new glass and poured from the bottle, liking the way her skirt fit across her ass way more than was good for him. His blood heated.

Desire.

It had been such a long time since he'd felt anything this potent, yet one look at Kelsey had blasted a beam of light right into the black hole of his libido.

Placing his glass in front of him, she said, 'So, why a cruise? If you're not a people person?'

Ari was pleased for his drink and took a deep swallow before he answered. 'I haven't had a vacation for a while and my boss' – Theo wasn't his boss but he'd be laughing his ass off to be described as such – 'ordered me to take leave. Something about it being unhealthy.'

'How long is a while?'

'Three years.'

'Three years?' She stared at him with wide eyes. 'Your boss is a wise man.'

Ari grunted. 'Please, the man doesn't need his ego fed any more.'

She laughed. 'I once worked back-to-back contracts, no break for eighteen months, and that nearly killed me.'

'I guess it's different for you. Being in close quarters with everyone all the time, not getting to go *home* at the end of the day. I get to go home.'

To his empty apartment. His empty bed. His empty life. No wonder he'd slept in his office a bit too much these past two years.

'Yeah, that part is hard. I miss my mum.'

Somehow the fact she had a mum and *missed* her made Kelsey that much more three-dimensional, and he suddenly wanted to know more about this woman who'd blown into his life and disrupted everything.

Up until Kelsey, Talia had been the only woman to make an impact on his life and Ari had no idea how to feel about that realisation.

'So why a cruise?' she asked, absently polishing the gleaming wood of the bar with a dry cloth.

It was only just starting to dawn on Ari how poorly he was cut out for lying. And how much he didn't want to be dishonest with Kelsey. But...

'My brother,' he said, gathering himself, 'suggested it was the perfect way to get away from *everything*, and when I looked online, this ship was sailing soon around the Greek Islands – only the best spot in the whole world even if I do say so myself.'

He smiled and she returned it, which emphasised the bow of her mouth and made him think about kissing it.

Kissing her.

'And it still had cabins available' – which it *shouldn't*, hence him being here – 'so I thought I'd check it out.'

'Most people don't' – she paused for a second as if she was trying to find a delicate way to word her statement – 'cruise alone.'

He shrugged. 'I don't mind my own company.'

'Yeah but it's a *cruise*. They're the very definition of a plus one. Hell, most people travel with multiple family and friends on these things.'

'Are you implying I'm a sad lonely dude with no friends?'

Ari kept his voice light but it wasn't that far from the truth. He'd pushed everyone away these past few years. His family had been a constant presence in his life whether he'd wanted it or not – and he had mostly not – but his UK friends had faded away since his return to Greece.

Not that he blamed them. They had tried to reach out but he'd rebuffed them at every turn.

She laughed then and it was like sunshine streaming through the portholes. 'I'm saying you might have had more fun with company.'

Ari hadn't come for fun but it'd sure as hell found him – or a version of it anyway. And guilt had kicked his ass ever since.

A telltale pink flush streaked across her cheeks as if she'd just realised what she'd said could be easily misconstrued, and he rushed in to alleviate her embarrassment. 'I'm having fun,' he said. 'This is my fun face.'

One elegant eyebrow kicked up at him. 'I think you might need to practise that one a little harder.'

Yeah. Ari hadn't had a lot of practice these past few years.

'So,' she said, deftly changing the subject, 'what *were* you thinking about? When I first came on?'

Ari thanked God it hadn't been her and he didn't have to lie again. He told her what he'd observed at dinner and how much it bothered him. 'Does that happen often?' he asked. 'Preferential treatment?'

'Sometimes, yes.' Her voice was low and Ari leaned in a little. 'It's not right but when tips can make such a big difference to your income it doesn't take some staff long to suss out who are the best tippers. I usually make a few extra thousand per contract from tip money so it can be worth it.'

Ari whistled. That was a nice bit of bonus cash – no wonder Sameel had been so obsequious. 'Still... it doesn't seem like a practice the cruise line should be encouraging, does it?'

'I wouldn't say it was encouraged. It's more... not consistently *dis*couraged. It's definitely frowned upon but the newer members of staff are often just modelling behaviours they see from the more senior members of staff.'

Which confirmed what Ari had thought about staff culture.

'And you don't find that disturbing?' *Just how deep did this vein of bad service run?*

'Of course, it's terrible.' Her voice was full of warm indignation. 'I grew up in a working-class suburb with a single mother who always struggled to make ends meet. I've seen her treated like a second-class citizen more times than I care to remember. But like in any workplace, there are people who do the right thing and people who do the wrong thing and all I can do is be responsible for my own behaviour.'

Ari nodded. It was true, of course, in every work environment, both good and bad could be found. Which included him at the moment. What he was doing now – using Kelsey for information – wasn't exactly exemplary behaviour.

Sure, they weren't in a relationship. They were a one-time thing which *had not* been motivated by his need for inside information. But still... it didn't feel right.

Just then a large group of people entered the bar, laughing loudly. They'd obviously been out for the day and had had a very good time. They were also obviously looking for somewhere to continue having a good time. Kelsey glanced at them uneasily for a brief moment, flicking her gaze from them to him and back to them again as they called her by name and she plastered a smile on her face.

Ari took that as his signal to leave, draining his glass and slipping off the stool as the crowd took over the bar.

* * *

Kelsey was tired and her feet were killing her as she plucked the pink cocktail umbrella out of the last empty glass, loaded it into the industrial dishwasher and pushed the on button. The Aphrodite Lounge had shut at midnight and, twenty minutes later, the staff were ready to knock off and grab a few hours' shut eye before turning up bright-eyed and bushy-tailed for the breakfast shift in the dining room.

Such was life on board a cruise ship. Long days, early starts, living where you worked. A day off here and there, shore leave every now and then. The constant awareness of the shifting blue mass underfoot and the steady presence of the far horizon.

She was looking forward to a shower and bed. Or at least her brain was. Her body was buzzing. Ari had walked into the lounge at eleven and sat in one of the chairs that faced the dance floor where a DJ was spinning some tunes to the younger crowd.

Thoughts of Ari had her picking up the umbrella, twisting it slowly in her fingers. He hadn't sat in her serving area so they hadn't exchanged any words. But hell if they hadn't eye-fucked each other for an hour.

She'd been excruciatingly aware of his hot gaze as it had tracked her around the busy lounge. Had felt it on her back and her ass and her tits. He hadn't openly ogled, it had been discreet, but she'd *known*.

She'd been aware, too, of the number of women who had approached him, who had smiled and flirted and asked him to dance. Aware of how unsettled it had made her when they did and how damn horny it had made her when he rebuffed every single one.

It shouldn't be a turn on. Who Ari did or did not dance with meant nothing to her, but she'd felt every polite shake of his head in her goddamn ovaries.

He'd sat on one whisky for the duration and she'd found herself wondering about whisky kisses. She'd stared at his mouth so often she'd committed it to memory. He'd caught her mid-stare more than once and their gazes had fused and melted and her nipples had tingled and her breath had caught and how she hadn't dropped trays she had no idea.

God... What was it with this guy?

She'd sworn after Eric she wasn't going to be distracted by a guy ever again. She had plans and commitments on the other side of the world. Very soon her mother's health was going to command all her attention – in *Australia*.

She didn't need this kind of distraction. They were supposed to be one and done, damn it.

But there was a hum in her blood and a buzz low in her belly that was hard to ignore and despite how tired she was, Kelsey didn't hold out much hope for a restful sleep.

Deciding to go for a turn around the ship to try and blow away some of the sexual frustration, Kelsey stepped out onto the top deck, the cocktail umbrella still in hand. It was deserted out here after midnight, nothing but the light breeze and the moon playing across the Med.

She walked for a bit, following the running track that circled the top deck before pocketing the umbrella and stopping to lean on the railing, staring out over the dark expanse of water disappearing into the inky night.

Kelsey loved working on cruise ships. She loved that every day – as she'd told Ari when they'd first met – she had a view of the ocean, which was as essential to her as breathing. She loved chatting with passengers and she adored the friendships and the sense of community amongst the staff.

But she needed to go home every now and then. Get her land legs. See her mother. And, after seven years in the industry, she was looking forward to the day she could call it quits. She certainly couldn't go for three years without a break as Ari had confessed to this afternoon.

Who even did that? Surely no one loved spreadsheets that much?

In fact, Ari didn't look like the kind of guy who was into spreadsheets at all. He looked like he sailed yachts and played polo and was the face of some expensive male cologne.

'A penny for them.'

Kelsey's breath cut out just above her vocal cords as the dark, rich voice so achingly familiar reached her in the night. As if she'd conjured him, Ari slid in beside her, leaning on the rail, also looking out to sea. His arm brushed hers, his hip mere inches away, and he smelled like whisky and maple syrup and forbidden freaking fruit.

Her pulse tripped. The nerve endings buried deep between her hips quivered.

'Santorini's out there somewhere,' Kelsey said, her voice husky because no way in hell was she admitting to thinking about him.

'Sea day tomorrow.'

'Yep.' Kelsey didn't look at him, too aware of his closeness and his heat and the way his voice wrapped around her. 'All hands on deck tomorrow.'

Even the thought of it made her weary. Sea days were crazy busy for the crew. Passengers loved the idea of relaxing all day but that didn't mean they didn't want to be constantly fed and watered and entertained. If she thought she was exhausted now, that would go double this time tomorrow night.

'You sound tired,' he said.

Kelsey swore he leaned into her a little more, the sweet intoxication of his scent filling her nostrils and going straight to her head. 'It's been a long day.'

'It has.'

'My feet are aching, I need a shower and I have to be up in five hours. I should be in my bed.'

She should not be out here with Ari George – with a *passenger*. Her heart fluttering like crazy, her fingers gripping the railing for fear she might shove them through his hair and yank him into a kiss.

'I have a shower.' His voice was a low rumble, just a touch louder than the muffled rumble of the ship's engines.

Kelsey's breath hitched and she braved a glance at him. His profile was strongly etched despite the night, the waves of his dark hair ruffling in the breeze. 'Ari.'

She didn't know if it was warning or encouragement. She didn't know jack any more.

'I've also been known to give excellent foot rubs.' His head turned and their gazes met, his as inky and deep as the Med at night. 'With or without a happy ending.'

'Ari...' Damn it, why must he be so damn irresistible? Why must he even be here at all? 'Were you waiting for me out here, for this?'

'No.' He shook his head. 'I came out here to cool my heels. Trying to ignore this compulsion I seem to have around you.'

Kelsey's ovaries jettisoned a surge of oestrogen at the ragged admission. He didn't seem to be particularly happy about it, his mouth a tight line, but it curled Kelsey's toes nonetheless.

'And then... here you were.'

Yeah. Here she was. Here *they* were. The universe seemed determined to put Ari in her path. Kelsey swallowed. 'We're supposed to be a one-time thing, remember?' Her voice felt high and tight in her throat but sounded like lead as it hit the air.

'I know.' He nodded and, for a moment, he looked as lost and bewildered by this thing as she did. 'But I can't seem to stop wanting you.'

His words squeezed big handfuls of her gut even though he clearly wasn't happy about them either, his inner conflict palpable. But his body turned towards her and she mirrored the action before she could stop herself. He was close – so close – his heat *everywhere* as his hand lifted slowly from the railing.

Kelsey shivered as his fingertips touched down on her jaw, tracing along it, her scalp prickling with sensation. His gaze followed the path of his fingers as they trailed down her throat, stopping at the hollow at the base, his eyes lifting, seeking hers.

Her breath stuttered to a halt; her nipples tightened. He was going to kiss her and she should pull back, she should walk away, but her body, already revelling in his touch, was now clamouring for his taste.

She moaned when his lips touched down, firm and good, hot and seeking. She couldn't help it or stop it; it came from a place of longing buried so deep she'd forgotten it had even existed. Whisky infused her senses and Kelsey gave into the madness, licked into his mouth, chased the flavour on his tongue and the deep resonance of his groan for long heady seconds.

Her pulse tripped and skipped and jumped all over, her breathing was reduced to wild breathless pants until sanity intruded and she wrenched away. They should not be kissing out here where anyone could stumble across them. They stared at each other for long moments, a charge between them, their breathing ragged.

'One more night,' he whispered.

God... it was *so* tempting. He was *so* tempting. Did Kelsey follow the rules or the wild beat of her heart? And the threats of mutiny coming from her vagina?

Her vagina won.

'Go to your room,' she said, her voice a husky pant. 'I'll be there in ten.'

It wasn't like she hadn't already committed an indiscretion, right? Might as well be hung for a sheep as a lamb...

6

Skulking along the passageways, Kelsey arrived at Ari's door exactly ten minutes later. She'd lifted her hand to knock but noticed it had been chocked open, so she pushed. Stepping inside, she was aware of two things instantly: the soft warm glow of the room and Ari standing at the end of the bed.

He was still fully dressed in the dark suit pants and graphite dress shirt he'd worn to dinner. The tie and jacket had come off, his sleeves had been rolled up to his elbows, but that was as far as his disrobing had gone.

'I thought you might change your mind,' he said, his eyes roving hot and rough over her body, picking up where they'd left off at the Aphrodite Lounge.

Kelsey shook her head, cleared her throat of the building huskiness. This whole thing might be crazy but, like Ari, she was having problems resisting. 'You promised me a shower.'

'I did.'

'I'd like to get wet now.'

He gestured in the direction of the bathroom. 'Wet is good.' A slight smile added to the intense obsidian of his gaze, and Kelsey felt it right between her legs.

Yeah... she didn't need a shower for that.

Kelsey contemplated crossing the distance and kissing him, but she didn't need a degree in human sexual interaction to know where *that* would lead.

And she *really* needed a shower. She stank of booze and bar nuts.

Without another word she turned and, kicking off her pumps as she went, disappeared into the bathroom. Quickly divesting herself of her clothes, she glanced at the mirror. Her green eyes glittered with what looked very much like anticipation.

'You are going to hell,' she mouthed to her reflection. It didn't reply, just stared back at her, very decidedly smug.

Kelsey leaned into the shower recess and flicked on the taps, adjusting them to the perfect degree of lukewarm. She looked over her shoulder. No Ari...

She frowned. She'd expected him to follow.

Kelsey took a step to the doorway to find him pouring himself a whisky. She placed her hands high on the door jamb as she caught his eye.

'Is there a reason you're still out here?'

His gaze took a slow tour of her body, lingering on all her good bits and causing quite the ruckus. The flare of his nostrils was intensely gratifying.

His gaze travelled back to her face. 'Not a lot of room in that shower.'

He made a good point. The cubicles weren't huge and Ari was a big guy, but she was willing to test the boundaries of the restricted space. 'I think we could manage it. Why don't you come wash my back and we'll see?'

He placed his glass on the table. 'Your wish is my command.'

She watched as he shucked his clothes in record time and fuck if he didn't look like a genie. Her own personal back washing, foot rubbing, well-endowed genie. All six-plus feet of him, gloriously naked, his cock out and proud in front. The ruckus in her good bits became a meltdown.

'I'll get the soap,' she said, a tad breathless as she turned away and stepped into the cubicle.

Warm water sluiced over her neck and shoulders as she reached for the bottle of liquid soap on the shelf attached to the wall. But then Ari's hand was sliding over the top of hers and his other hand was sliding onto her hip and his lips were sliding onto her neck and Kelsey's pulse doubled.

His front pressed into her back – hot and hard – and the granite of his cock pressed into the cleft of her buttocks as he pumped soap into his hand. Kelsey arched against him, one hand moving to anchor around his neck, the other dipping behind to grab a buttock.

'This is a great view,' he muttered near her ear as he angled her away from the direct spray, his soapy hand gliding onto her stomach.

Kelsey's abs clenched at the touch. 'That's not my back.'

'Patience,' he whispered, his hand circling her belly button. 'I'll get there.'

Kelsey moaned and arched some more as the muscles behind her navel undulated in wanton bliss. He was right. It was a fucking fantastic view.

Mesmerising.

His big hand looked even more bronzed on her pale flesh as it moved in slow circles, making bubbles and lighting fires in its wake. She watched as it moved slowly north and moaned as his other hand joined the action, both of them sliding onto her breasts, spreading bubbles in tandem.

She cried out as long fingers worked her slippery nipples into two taut peaks, giving a twist at each end for an added zing.

'You want me to stop and do your back?' he asked, his breathing heavy in her ear.

Kelsey gave a half laugh. 'If you stop I'll kill you.'

His low chuckle slid down her spine and undulated through the muscles deep inside her belly. She never wanted this to stop. She never wanted to get out of this shower. She wanted to say in here with him forever, giving and taking pleasure until the day she died.

No work, no money issues, no mother facing an ever-darkening world. No outside problems. Just him and her in this shower. In this cabin.

It was *all* the crazy but, right here, right now, nothing mattered other than Ari and what he was doing to her body.

'I think you're going to want some of this too,' he muttered, one hand heading south.

Kelsey protested the loss of nipple action for the two seconds it took for Ari's fingers to find her clitoris and then her objections were lost in a tsunami of sensation and the deep, sonorous moan that slipped unchecked from her lips.

'Oh, you *really* like that,' he said, licking down her neck.

'Stop and I'll *really* kill you.'

He didn't stop. He just stroked her clit over and over – firmly and deftly. His mouth was hot on her neck and his whiskers rasped like sandpaper as the fingers on her breast continued to tease with similar precision.

It was as if he knew her body. Or was, at least, attuned to its rhythms – sensitive to every moan, every wriggle, every back arch. Responsive to every nuance.

She'd been with men who were good in bed – knew the bases and were just as keen to give as they were to take. Guys who were more than happy to follow instructions when they weren't quite hitting the mark.

But Ari?

This shit seemed intuitive. He anticipated better than any man she'd ever known. It was like he was two paces ahead, giving her exactly what she needed, before she even knew she needed it.

Like sliding one finger, then two, inside her and pinching her nipple, taking her slow simmer to an instant boil, everything coiling tight for long seconds then flying loose.

Kelsey cried out, clamping down hard on his ass as she drowned in a hot wave of pleasure. Every nerve, every muscle, every *cell* lit up with it as she was sucked into the undertow gasping for air and drenched down to her bones.

She slumped against him as the climax dissipated and he eased his fingers from between her legs. Her hand slid from his ass and her arm around his neck went limp, and she was thankful for the powerful support of his quads as her knees threatened to buckle.

'Time to rinse,' he whispered in her ear, easing them around a little.

The hard spray from the shower hit her front and she gasped, her eyelids flying open. It wasn't cold but her skin was excruciatingly sensitive. The spray stung her nipples in a *good* way, and even the bubbles sliding off her body felt like tiny tongues lapping at her skin. For the love of all that was holy, how was she still so *aroused*?

When she could barely stand?

She must have whimpered because he shushed her and whispered, 'It's okay, shhh, I know. I'm not done yet.'

Then he slid from behind her, his cock still a rod of honed steel, the head flushed with arousal. He eased her back until her shoulder blades hit the tiles, and dropped to his knees, his mouth pressing hot kisses to her belly, along the crease where abdomen met leg, and over the tops of her thighs.

Kelsey glanced down. The sight of him kneeling before her made her legs even weaker. As did the proximity of his mouth to her pussy. She ploughed her hand through his hair and gave a tug, and those black eyes locked on hers.

'I'm not sure I can handle any more just now.' Her clit was always extraordinarily sensitive post orgasm.

'You can't handle a foot rub?' he asked with faux innocence.

Kelsey quirked an eyebrow. 'My feet are a lot lower than that.'

He grinned. 'Nothing wrong with spreading a little joy on the way down, is there?' He pressed a kiss to her belly button. 'You can stop me if it's too much.'

And then his hand was sliding onto the back of a thigh and lifting her leg, placing it over his shoulder until her heel grazed the centre of his back, opening her right up to him.

'*Theé*,' he muttered, his gaze fixed on her pussy as his other hand slid onto her ass.

He leaned in then, putting his mouth over her, the flat of his tongue finding her clit in one long slow lick that had her gasping. More long slow licks followed, a technique that was somehow both a balm to the poor tortured nub and a hot, throbbing stimulus even more potent than his finger.

Kelsey moaned, her ass cheeks clenching at the first pull of her approaching orgasm. Her pulse, barely recovered from last time, kicked into overdrive. What the hell?

She was going *again*? This *never* happened. But she was, *going again*. And she was going fast.

How could she be building so damn quickly when his tongue was moving so maddeningly slow? The rapid approach of her orgasm was so out of step with the unhurried pace of his tongue it was a turn on all on its own, a delicious kind of confusion.

The man was a freak.

He lifted his head, grinning up at her. 'How are you handling it? You need me to stop yet?'

Kelsey was in no state to humour him. She just grabbed the back of his head and jammed his face back into her pussy. His muffled laughter gave way to the hot stroke of his tongue and the almost instantaneous firing of a thousand tiny pulses, darting straight from her clit.

They travelled to her inner thighs, then her outer thighs. To her pelvis and on to her belly button. Gathering speed and strength and momentum until the climax fired off in one long contraction, rolling from her clit to her nipples.

'*Ari!*'

It was shorter than the last orgasm but more intense as Kelsey's hand twisted hard in his hair and her heel dug into his flesh. He was probably going to end up with a bruise in the centre of his back and a massive bald patch, but if she was inflicting any pain, he didn't complain. He just kept swiping the flat of his tongue against her clit until the climax spun away.

'Stop,' she panted, yanking on his hair, wrenching him away, her head falling back against the tiles. 'Enough.'

Kelsey watched him through half-closed lids as he rose like freaking Poseidon from the sea, all hard and male and potent as fuck. He had that smug kind of look she'd seen on her own face earlier, and she gave a half laugh because words weren't currently possible. Her eyes were working fine though and she watched, enthralled, as he ducked his head under the spray, water sluicing over his face and down his body.

'You have an extremely dextrous tongue,' she said, finally coherent enough to speak.

He grinned but shook his head. 'I'm a little rusty.'

Kelsey blinked. *Rusty?* Why was a guy, who was clearly a freak between the sheets, rusty? And if this was him *rusty*, how wrecked would she have been with his oral superpowers fully oiled?

Before she could reply, he flicked off the taps and reached for her, sliding an arm under her legs and one around her back, picking her up with ease. Kelsey might have objected had her legs not been jelly. But they were, so she looped her arms around his neck instead.

'What now?'

'I still have one more condom,' he said and strode from the shower.

* * *

Twenty minutes later, Ari lay boneless in the aftermath, Kelsey's legs intertwined with his, her tousled hair spread out on his chest. He slid a hand onto her hip, hitching her closer as his thumb stroked lazy swirls on the rounded flank of her upper thigh.

'I bet you couldn't do that again if you tried,' she said, propping her chin on his chest, her husky vibrato ruffling the air around his body.

Ari grinned. 'Sure I can. You might need to give me a second to recover.'

She laughed and it was light and happy and filled all the spaces inside him that had been so desolate for so long and it was nice being with her like this, lying in the aftermath all slow and lazy and thoroughly sated, idly touching, stroking.

He felt a resurgence of the guilt that had plagued him these past days, but it was quickly swallowed up by a sense of revelation. Who knew that he *could* feel this way again? That he could be intimate in *this* way – perhaps an even deeper form of intimacy than sex – with somebody else?

Ari honestly didn't know what to do with such a thought. It belonged in the hot mess of emotions that Kelsey had stirred up since they'd met.

'That move has a high degree of difficulty,' she said, her voice low and lazy as she traced circles on his collarbone. 'You practise that often?'

Ari's hand stopped its stroking. 'Are you fishing, Ms Armitage?'

'No.' She smiled. 'I'm letting you know my best friend also works on this ship. She can castrate a steer in ten seconds flat and I *will* send her to this cabin if you tell me you're using me to screw around on someone.'

Ari laughed – God, how long had it been since he'd laughed like this? – despite the abhorrence of her cheating implication.

He was a one-woman guy, always had been.

'You can tell your friend to stand down. There's nobody.'

Nobody. The thought was hardly new but it was sobering. Up until this cruise, Ari hadn't particularly cared. He hadn't looked outside his shell in three years.

Meeting Kelsey had him reassessing everything.

'Right answer,' she said, that cupid's bow stretching out as the smile spread across her face. Her finger stroked down his chin and along his jaw line, the faint rasp of his whiskers loud in the night.

'I had a wife...'

Her finger stopped in its tracks, the bow relaxed back to its usual fullness. She blinked. So did Ari. What the hell? He hadn't planned on saying that *at all*.

It had just... slipped out.

Ari didn't talk about Talia. He'd tried, in the beginning, but his family had discouraged it because it caused him distress. They'd thought it healthier to look forward, not back. So he'd stopped trying.

Hell, he'd barely opened up to his therapist about her.

But he *hadn't* moved forward. He'd talked to her in his head instead, shutting everyone out. Just him and her, holding her close that way.

'Okay.'

Ari liked that she wasn't battering him with questions or freaking out. That she was waiting for him to direct the conversation. 'She died. Three years ago. In a car accident. She was thirty.'

Her gaze searched his and Ari watched as realisation dawned across her face. 'The one you were in. That causes your migraines?'

'Yes.'

'I'm sorry.' She slid her hand onto his cheek, her fingers brushing his hairline. 'So very sorry. That's a truly shit thing to happen.'

Ari stared at her for a few seconds, taken aback by her unusual condolences. And then, much to his surprise, a big bubble of laughter rose in his chest and found its way out his mouth.

'Oh God, I'm sorry.' She leaned back a little, her cheeks turning pink, her brows crinkling in consternation. 'That wasn't very respectful, was it? I never really know what to say.'

'No.' Ari shook his head. 'It's perfect. I've heard so many well-meaning platitudes this past three years I want to scream. People telling me that "there's a reason for everything" and "at least she didn't suffer" or that "God needed another angel in heaven".'

He shook his head. He knew people were as much at a loss over something to say as Kelsey, but he'd rather they said nothing at all than something trite. He slid his hands onto her face, cupping her cheeks. 'It *was* shit and you have no idea how good it is to hear somebody say that.' Ari was glad he'd gone with the strange urge to open up. 'You clearly have a gift with words,' he teased, wanting to dissolve the frown knitting her brows together.

She gave him a crooked smile. 'Oh yeah. I should definitely open my own condolence card company.'

He laughed. 'Let me know if you ever need an investor.'

And then he kissed her, savouring her mouth for long, drugging moments. The scent of his soap on her skin and the feel of her breasts squashed against his chest was a dizzying combination.

He wanted this woman. Forbidden or not. Morally ambiguous or not. Risky or not. It made no sense. It just was.

But she broke away, the bow of her upper lip wet and a little swollen from his passion. 'Is that what you meant earlier?' she asked. 'About being rusty?'

'Yeah. There hasn't been anyone else.'

'Since she died? For *three* years?'

He nodded. The thought of being with anyone else after Talia had been about as exciting as a kick to the balls. 'Are you freaking out?'

'No.' She shook her head slowly. 'I'm... impressed.'

'By the period of celibacy?'

'Yes. And' – she smiled – 'your still-impressive skills. You're like a wizard or something.'

He laughed as she slid her leg over him and pushed herself up, straddling his hips. She was glorious astride him like this, her hair in disarray, her skin pale against the swarthier tone of his, her rose-tipped breasts full and round and bouncy.

Gathering her hair to the side, she leaned in to kiss him and Ari met her halfway, raising his head off the pillow, kissing her quick and hard. She moaned as he stroked his tongue against hers and desire flowed like quicksilver through his veins and flooded his groin, his cock stiffening in an instant.

'Mmm,' she murmured against his mouth as she rubbed herself up and down his length. 'You brought your magic wand, I see.'

He chuckled, his hands stroking down her back to her ass, holding her tight against him. 'What self-respecting wizard leaves home without it?'

She ground a little harder, moaning in a way that went straight to his testicles. 'It's indefatigable, isn't it?'

'It is,' Ari muttered, dropping a chain of kisses from the side of her mouth to her ear. After three years of celibacy, his cock had returned with impressive vigour. 'Unfortunately for it, I'm out of condoms.'

Ari hadn't thought to secure more. Because they weren't supposed to be doing this again.

'Oh no,' she whispered, dropping her head to the side. 'The poor thing.'

'He's very sad,' Ari murmured, nuzzling down her neck, his tongue licking against the pulse fluttering in her throat.

'Maybe I can kiss him better?'

Ari's groin tightened. 'I'm sure he'd enjoy that.'

He kissed her then, hard and deep one more time before Kelsey broke away and moved determinedly *south*. Down his throat, buzzing her lips and flicking her tongue over his nipples, licking around his belly button, tracing the trail of hair heading south from his navel all the way down to the root of his cock.

Ari groaned as she grabbed hold around the base and planted a string of kisses the length of his shaft all the way to the tip. When she reached the flushed taut crown, she licked at the bead of liquid that had formed at the slit and Ari's hands bunched in the sheets.

The urge to thrust up, to push himself into her mouth, rode him like the devil. He wanted to see her lips stretched around him, he wanted to feel the head of his cock pushing into the soft give at the back of her throat, and he wanted to lock gazes with her as she sucked and released every inch of him.

But he didn't. Because most of all he wanted to prolong this connection. Not just the wet suck of her mouth but the intimacy of the act. When he'd gone to that other woman's room so long ago, he'd wanted two things – to forget and for it to be over.

It was different with Kelsey. He wanted to remember every moment and he never wanted it to end.

Ari didn't know how he was going to feel about this time when it was all over – he expected it wasn't going to be pretty – but right now he felt alive, and that felt good.

Slowly – oh so slowly – her mouth sunk down over his taut, aching girth, wet and hot and *so fucking good*, he almost went blind with the flare of light bursting across his retina. It was pure torture to stay still, not to place his hand on the back of her head and thrust.

Ari's balls tightened and the nerves at the base of his spine sparked and lit up like a circuit board. He groaned as her cheeks hollowed out on the upstroke, his hands tightening in the sheets as she sucked good and hard. Pausing at the head, she swirled her tongue around and around, lingering each time on the underside, flicking back and forth against the ridge of skin before completing another full rotation and doing it again.

Theé! She was the devil!

He grunted as her tongue relented its maddening flick and she plunged her mouth down his shaft once more, their gazes locking. Kelsey's big green eyes stared at him through strands of her hair as he bottomed out and her throat worked to accommodate him, moving convulsively, moisture glistening at the corners of her mouth as she held him there for interminable seconds.

Christe! Her mouth was pure, wicked sin.

She half gasped, half gagged as she finally withdrew. But not fully; she spent long moments torturing the taut aching crown again, her eyes fixed on his, the muscles in his ass clamped tight as wheel nuts. She dallied mercilessly, stoking the spreading heat in his belly before heading south again, taking him all the way to the back, swallowing convulsively again, humming her desire as she held.

The low guttural sound vibrated right through his testicles and they pulled even tighter as cool fingers dragged up the centre of his ball sack, cupping and squeezing. The sensation was like throwing rocket fuel on the fire of his arousal and Ari groaned, praying for strength.

'Theé dóse mou dýnami.'

Pulling off him, one hand still firmly at the base of his cock, Kelsey's mouth found his balls. The wet heat was a shocking contrast to her cool fingers and Ari's hips bucked involuntarily. When she sucked first one and then the other in her mouth, the muscles of his ass locked so tight he was pretty sure he was going to need some kind of intravenous medication to relax them again.

Ari closed his eyes as she rolled them in the hot cavern of her mouth and saw stars – tiny, white pinpricks of light bursting into supernovas as her tongue savoured them like they were the finest damn truffles in the land. His heart beat like it never had before, and there was a tightness in his chest that made him breathless and restless all at once. Lightning forked up his spine and sizzled along nerve endings.

She made him want to cuss and buck and grind. She made him want to split his skin. She made him want to give in to the desperate urge to let go.

Just when Ari felt certain he couldn't contain his orgasm any longer, Kelsey's tongue trekked from his balls to the crown again and sunk down. But she didn't play around this time. She didn't tease or do clever things with her tongue. She just sucked him – all the way down and all the way up, applying just the right amount of suction.

And as his climax rushed out from his groin and wrung through the muscles of his ass and thighs and belly, Ari *couldn't* keep his hands still any longer – he *had* to touch. His fingers slid into her hair, glorying at the silky strands as he cupped her head, crying out as the first jet of come roared from his balls straight into the wet, willing heat of her mouth.

She moaned as her throat worked to hold him deep and swallow at the same time, the sound sinking hot talons into his ass. And then her hand closed tight around his balls and flaming arrows of lust let fly, finding their marks with pinpoint precision.

Ari's body was one giant throb. His abdomen pulsed, his groin pulsed, the thick, fat vein at his neck pulsed. The mad flutter at his temples was loud in his ears. His entire body trembled to the hard drumbeat of his heart.

And then it was over, the climax ebbing and finally stealing away, leaving him spent and ravaged, his breathing heavy as Kelsey planted tiny kisses from the soft, vulnerable skin of his groin to the dip of his belly button, to the flat brown discs of his nipples.

Reaching his throat, she nuzzled her way along the ridge of his trachea before anchoring her bent elbow snug in his armpit and propping her head on her hand. She quirked an eyebrow. 'Does he feel better now?'

Ari chuckled, his hand sliding up her back, under the golden strands of her hair to her shoulder. 'I think it's fair to say he feels fucking fantastic.'

She smiled. 'Then my work here is done.'

7

Kelsey tiptoed through the deserted passageway to her cabin like a thief in the night. In half an hour it would be bustling with staff busily heading to the breakfast shift but for now, it was all clear.

She'd hadn't meant to stay the night with Ari. Kelsey didn't usually *stay the night*. Since Eric had screwed her over so thoroughly, she'd been determined not to get close to anyone, not to let anyone distract her from her goals.

Once the sexy times were done – she left. Sleeping with someone was *relationship* territory. Not one-night-stand territory. And definitely not ill-advised, against-the-rules cruise *fling* territory.

And she'd gotten the distinct impression the last time she'd been in Ari's bed that he'd been relieved when she'd scrambled out of it and gone back to her quarters.

But she must have been even more exhausted than she'd thought and by the time she realised Ari had drifted to sleep she was almost there herself, and it was so warm and snuggly by his side.

Kelsey smiled then shook her head. She should not be smiling at five fifteen in the morning. She'd had less than three hours' sleep and was acutely aware of the ache between her legs and the graze just above her left nipple from a string of over-zealous kisses. But every part of her hummed with satisfaction and just thinking about the pink paper umbrella she'd found in her pocket and left on Ari's vanity unit turned her smile goofy.

Not even the thought she'd broken another rule and stayed the night was enough to stop her smiling.

Grabbing her swipe card, Kelsey waved it in front of her door and quietly pushed it open, grateful for the single cabin that came with being a senior member of staff. She didn't want to have to face any roomie questions.

But she wasn't counting on Tiffany being around.

'Well, hello there.'

Kelsey practically jumped out of her skin, turning to find Tiffany leaning casually against the door jamb of her cabin next door. 'Jesus,' she hissed. 'Must you *lurk*?'

A fiercely imperious eyebrow – Tiff's eyebrows were magnificent – winged halfway up Tiffany's forehead. 'I'm not lurking, I'm just getting off shift.'

She indicated her croupier uniform that hugged all her curves and had caused many a punter to lose his mind and his chips. The other eyebrow winged upwards. 'What's your excuse?'

Crap. What *was* her excuse? 'I... wanted to see the sunrise.'

'In your uniform from last night?' Tiffany laughed as if it was the most absurd thing she'd ever heard.

Kelsey shushed her before dragging her into her cabin and shutting the door. 'Do you want to wake everybody up?' she demanded.

Those eyebrows knitted together as Tiffany eyed her speculatively. 'You're having *sex*.'

'No.' Kelsey's denial was hot and fast but the instantaneous shot of colour to her cheeks gave her away.

'Oh my God.' Tiffany grinned. 'You *are*, aren't you?'

Kelsey's second denial was significantly weaker. 'You're being ridiculous.'

But Tiffany in full sleuth mode was not to be deterred. 'It's that new sommelier, isn't it? Damon or Devon or something?'

'Davida,' Kelsey supplied. Tiffany's shocking memory for names was legendary. 'And no. I'm not screwing any of the wait staff.'

She snapped her fingers. 'That hottie dancer dude with the tight buns and a twelve pack? The blond one.'

'No.' There was significant male talent amongst the entertainment staff but Kelsey doubted she could ever sleep with a blond again after being with the bronzed and beautiful Ari.

Tiffany narrowed her eyes. 'Why are you being so evasive? You're never evasive.' Suddenly, her face took on a look of abject horror. 'Oh dear God, you're not screwing one of the officers, are you? You know those dudes are the biggest manwhores in existence.'

A few years ago, their friend Jamilla had been screwed over by a first officer and Tiffany had to be restrained from putting a cockroach in his dinner.

'No. Jesus, Tiff, take a breath.'

'You're sleeping with someone, Kels. I know you. You're a lousy liar. You're slinking back to your cabin at daybreak and blushing like a virgin.'

Kelsey blushed again and those eyebrows rose in an *I-told-you-so* expression. Tiffany plonked herself down on the bed and patted the empty mattress beside her. 'Spill, woman. You know you want to.'

She did. Kelsey wanted desperately to confide in her best friend. She wanted to tell Tiffany about Ari, about this crazy hot attraction that flared like a torch every time she saw him.

Every time she thought about him.

Even now, her body awash with satisfaction from their night together, she craved his touch. Maybe talking about this insanity would give her the push she needed to exorcise him from her system.

Kelsey sank onto the bed beside Tiffany. 'It's not an officer or one of the dancers. It's... a passenger.'

Tiffany blinked, momentarily speechless. But she was never silenced for long. 'Fuckin' hell, Kels. Since when do *you* screw the passengers? I mean, me... sure. Been there, done that. Hell, I reckon half of us have at one stage or other, but you've *never* gone there.'

'It's only been twice. And it's not happening again.' Saying it out loud was like the kind of finality she needed. Even if it did feel like a punch to her gut.

Tiffany grinned wickedly and clapped her hands like a kid on

Christmas morning. 'Oh my God, tell me *everything*. Who is he? What does he do? Does he have an enormous dong?'

Kelsey almost choked on her laughter. 'You are incorrigible. And a terrible influence. You should be lecturing me about the perils of such a liaison. Hell, Tiff, you should be *reporting* me!'

'Oh, fuck that, lovie. I'm on team Kelsey and life's too damn short not to get naked and horizontal at every opportunity.'

'I could get *fired*.'

'Only if you're not discreet. Now please tell me he's exceptionally good at giving head.'

Another laugh threatened to strangulate mid-throat. 'His name is Ari. He's Greek but he actually sounds very English. He was educated there and lived in London for a decade. He's an accountant and has an inner cabin on deck seven. And yes.' Kelsey paused for dramatic effect. 'The man eats pussy like a freaking ninja.'

Tiffany laughed and hugged her. 'Go you! You're practically glowing. How did it start?'

Kelsey gave the abridged version considering she had to get ready for work. About Andy and the wallet and the stolen money. 'It's been crazy, Tiff. And the sex...'

Kelsey didn't know if there was a word in the entire English *or Greek* language adequate enough to describe the sex, so she didn't bother.

'And he's interesting and kind.' The fact he got so riled up about Sameel treating passengers differently spoke volumes about Ari's character. 'And he's so... tactile. Playing with my hair or stroking my skin.'

Kelsey had been surprised to find she liked being petted. It was crazy to think in a few days she'd let a guy she barely knew closer than any man had been in years.

'Well, good for you.' Tiffany squeezed Kelsey's hand.

'We're not doing it again. It's too risky.' How anyone risked it, Kelsey had no idea. She was not cut out for this kind of subterfuge.

'I don't care,' Tiffany said. 'I'm still stalking his ass. You're going to have to point him out to me. How old is he?'

'I... don't know.' Kelsey laughed, slightly mortified that she had no clue. It wasn't like they hadn't talked about deeply personal stuff. 'He'd have to be early thirties I suppose. He went to uni and lived in London for a decade. He and his wife were in a car crash three years ago and she was thirty at the time so...'

'His wife? Divorced?'

Kelsey shook her head. 'Widower.'

'Oh God.' Tiffany's expressive eyebrows knitted close, her palm flattened over her chest. 'That's awful.'

'Yes.' Kelsey had been ten when her dad had died and that had taken a piece of her heart she'd never get back. 'I'm the first one, Tiff. The first woman he's been with since his wife.'

The frown on her best friend's face deepened. 'You're his *first*? Since his wife died?'

Kelsey's scalp prickled at the thread of alarm in her friend's voice. 'Yes.'

'Oh no.' Tiffany shook her head. 'No, no, no, Kels.' She stood and started pacing the cabin. 'That's a *bad* idea.'

'Yeah. I already *know* that. Against the rules, remember. That's why we're not doing it again.'

'No, I mean—' Tiffany stopped pacing and faced Kelsey. 'You're transition woman.'

Kelsey's frown deepened. 'What?'

'Men don't fall for transition woman, Kels.' Tiffany folded her arms impatiently. 'You're... practice.'

'Tiff... you're not listening. It's just sex. And it's not happening again.'

Her eyebrows almost hit her hairline this time. 'Bullshit it's just sex. You're *glowing*, babe. You're talking about how kind and interesting and *touchy* he is when usually you're counting down the minutes until you can leave. Face it, babe, you're... smitten.'

Kelsey almost choked. 'Smitten?' That was preposterous. 'Did I fall down a rabbit hole and land in the nineteenth century?'

Tiffany pursed her lips. 'It's the perfect word.'

'I'm not.' Kelsey shook her head vigorously. 'It's sex. Great sex, admittedly, but that's it. And we're done.'

'Oh God.' Tiffany gave her a hard hug. 'You're going to get your heart squashed.'

Kelsey laughed at the drama. 'I'm not falling in love with him. We had sex, now it's over. I'm going to be fine.'

She would be fine, damn it.

Breaking out of her friend's boa constrictor-like embrace, Kelsey said, 'I need a shower, and you' – she poked Tiff's chest – 'you need a sleep. You're clearly overtired.'

'Don't say I didn't warn you.'

Kelsey rolled her eyes. 'Duly noted. Now go.'

The door clicked shut behind Tiffany and Kelsey breathed a sigh of relief. *Transition woman?* Tiffany always did have a flare for the dramatic.

* * *

Ari didn't know how he felt as he left his cabin at nine for breakfast. He'd woken alone but feeling good, feeling happy, and he couldn't think why for a beat or two until the scent of Kelsey rose from his sheets and the taste of her lingered on his lips, and he remembered drifting to sleep with her by his side.

How long she'd stayed in his bed he didn't know, but her body had been limp and heavy against his and he was sure she'd drifted off too. Two nights ago he'd been tense about her falling asleep and last night, it hadn't even crossed his mind as his sated body had slipped into slumber.

He'd slept with another woman. And woken up with a smile on his face.

Which was confusing as fuck.

It wasn't that he woke up crushingly sad and weighed down by helplessness any more. Even the boiling rage he'd felt in every cell of his body had passed. It was the absence of feeling that had haunted him for the last couple of years.

The numbness.

No joy or happiness. No excitement. No lightness or colour. No sadness or anger, either. Just him, flatlining his way through life. And then a girl – a *woman* – on a ship had put a cocktail umbrella in his whisky and he'd come alive.

Ari couldn't deny it despite how much his heart demanded he do so. He'd actually laughed when he'd seen that pink umbrella sitting on his vanity unit this morning. *Laughed*. It'd been a long time since he'd laughed in the morning.

A vice clamped tight around his chest at the thought of things changing after so long. It made him edgy and jittery, and Ari shook his head and forced himself to concentrate on the day ahead. On why he was here. He had a full schedule, and letting himself be distracted by things he had no answers for wasn't productive.

Today was a sea day as they steamed towards Santorini, which meant he had a full day on board to poke around the ship. First port of call was a visit to the ship hospital with a bogus gastro-intestinal complaint to see if quarantine protocols were being followed.

Ari assumed they weren't being rigidly adhered to what with the recent outbreaks of norovirus on several of their cruises. Given how fast the virus spread and the elder demographic of their passengers, it was not an area where cruise ship companies could be lax.

After he'd been to the hospital, he'd check out the various activities run by the ship. There were several sessions of trivia and karaoke per day and a daily bingo game where some serious money could be won. There were a couple of lectures taking place in the theatre – one on the formation of the Greek islands by a geology lecturer and another about the gods and goddesses of Greek culture by a mythology professor. And a Martini-making class was happening in one of the bars.

In short, he had a big day.

No time to be mooning over cocktail umbrellas, sexy Australian waitresses and psychoanalysing what the fuck was happening.

* * *

After breakfast, he headed straight to the medical clinic. The *Hellenic Spirit* was fitted with a state of the art mini hospital. Among other things there was an operating theatre, a fully equipped intensive care bed and a helipad on the top deck for medical evacs.

They should have been able to handle something as trivial – although just as potentially disastrous – as a gastro bug. Sadly, this was not the case as he reported his non-existent gastro symptoms right out of the norovirus handbook. Nausea, vomiting, stomach cramps, diarrhoea.

It should have triggered the GE protocol Ari knew every ship had adopted. It didn't.

Sure, the staff manning the clinic were brisk and efficient and professional, but their 'recommendation' that Ari rest in his cabin for the day, drink plenty of liquids and come back and see them tomorrow if he was still experiencing symptoms was not stringent enough.

It should have been a medical order.

He should have been placed into immediate *mandatory* cabin quarantine with a member of the medical team ringing him to check in every two hours during the day and every four hours overnight. Both for his welfare and to ensure he was adhering to the quarantine protocols and not being his own one-man Typhoid Mary band.

Much to Ari's dismay, none of those things were insisted upon. Nor was he followed up during the day to ensure he'd been adhering to the recommendations. They had his phone number and had he not answered they should have gone to his cabin to confirm he was following the quarantine measures and check on his wellbeing. Discovering him not there should have resulted in him being paged through the ship's PA system.

He was not. And Ari was not pleased.

The activities impressed him, however, and by and large, most of what he saw throughout the day cheered him. The staff had bought their A game and all the passengers seemed in fine spirits. He made a point to chat to random people throughout the day, gently enquiring as to their experiences on the ship, and they'd all been complimentary.

But that all ended at dinner. Once again, he'd been placed at an entirely different table from the previous night. This one was nowhere in line of sight of Kelsey's section – a very good thing for his concentration. The food was its usual high quality and the waiter on the table – Prishna – restored Ari's faith in the Ōceanós training manual.

He appeared to be about the same age as Sameel but was polite, generous and efficient whilst treating everyone the same. There was no preferential treatment for the one American couple at the table – he treated all his customers as if they were kings and queens.

Ari made a note to add Prishna's name to the list of staff members he was going to single out for praise.

Sadly, the same could not be said for Jean Paul, the suave, silver-fox maître d'. He'd been scurrying around all night being generally smooth and charming, making the women giggle in faux outrage at his jokes and flattering male egos left, right and centre. But it was what Ari saw as he was leaving the restaurant that boiled his blood.

Distracted by the double whammy of pleasant memories and nagging guilt, as he'd been on numerous occasions today, he almost missed the incident and would have altogether had he not been forced to step around a group of people who'd decided to stop in the middle of the dining room for a chat. His diverted path took him close by the entrance to the kitchen which had been artfully disguised by a couple of large potted palms.

Because of Ari's angle and proximity though, the plants did not mask Jean Paul just inside the kitchen door, pressing himself against one of the waitresses. The act was clearly unwelcome as she twisted her face away to avoid his lips and, when he groped her breast, she pushed at him, escaping his hold and scurrying out the kitchen through the door at the opposite end to where Ari was standing.

It took a few seconds for what Ari had seen to compute. To realise he had actually just witnessed a senior male staff member of great power and esteem assaulting a junior female member of staff.

At work.

With a restaurant full of people surrounding him.

A nerve ticked in Ari's eye and a blood vessel throbbed in his temple. *Gamoto.* The arrogance of the man that he would do something so awful and so *openly* was stunning.

He obviously knew he could get away with it.

Rapidly prioritising his actions, Ari hurried to check on Jean Paul's victim first. He spotted her darting out the main door. 'Miss,' he called after her. When she didn't respond, Ari put on a burst of speed and called 'Miss' again, as he grabbed her arm to stall her flight.

She turned, her big brown eyes large in her face. She was slight with skinny arms and barely looked twenty. 'Luzviminda,' Ari said, reading her nametag, hoping he was pronouncing it correctly. 'Are you okay?'

She nodded, but she was trembling, reminding Ari of a scared little bird. 'I saw what happened... back there, at the restaurant. That's not okay.'

'Is fine,' she said, her voice small as she forced a smile on her face that looked both miserable and petrified. 'Nothing happen. I want no trouble.'

Ari eased his hand away in case he was scaring her more. 'I'm sorry,' he said, keeping his voice gentle. 'I'm not trying to scare you. My name is Ari. Ari George, I'm a passenger and I saw what he did to you. You need to report it.'

Her eyes grew to the size of saucers. 'Oh no.' She shook her head vehemently. 'I just need break.'

'He's not allowed to do that to you. I will report him if you don't.'

Ari just couldn't let this go, no matter how much poor Luzviminda wanted him to.

'Oh no, please... Is okay.' Her eyes swam with tears as she appealed to Ari. 'I can't lose job. My family... I send money home.'

And Ari would bet his last cent Jean Paul knew it too. The blood vessel in his temple moved dangerously close to popping.

'Has he done this before?'

She shook her head again. 'Please... I okay.' Then she whirled away, walking as fast as she could from Ari and the dining room without drawing any attention to herself.

Ari's fists clenched by his sides as his blood pulsed at his temples. That... bastard. That slimy, detestable sonofabitch. How could he do that to someone he owed a duty of care?

He wanted to storm into the kitchen and plant his fist right in that smug asshole's face. And kick him in the balls while he was down. Give Jean Paul a full demonstration of how it is to feel weak and vulnerable and powerless. How it is to have someone touch you in private places without your permission.

But he knew if he went in there now and sacked him on the spot, threw his weight around, he'd blow his cover. Not to mention give that sleazy bastard a reason to launch legal action for assault if the urge to hit him got the better of Ari.

So he did the next best thing. Luzviminda might not feel that she had a voice, but he certainly did and Jean Paul's days were up. Ari withdrew his phone from his jacket pocket and dialled Theo's number.

* * *

The staff were abuzz the next morning with the news of Jean Paul's sacking. Of course, the HR team didn't say exactly *why*, only that the long-time maître d' had been let go after a 'passenger complaint of misconduct'. He'd been dismissed forthwith and would be leaving the ship at Santorini.

The second in charge, a Venezuelan guy called Ramon, who was efficient, well liked and *not sleazy*, had been promoted effective immediately.

Kelsey glanced out the nearest porthole as she trekked to a table who had requested more coffee. The majestic spine of Santorini rose out of the deep blue volcanic cauldron in which it sat. The whitewashed houses dazzled in the sun, their iconic blue roofs like sirens to cashed-up tourists.

The iron tracks of the cable car glinted in the sunshine and, at the bottom of the cobblestone road that zigzagged up to the village of Fira, donkeys and their masters waited patiently for the passengers who had forked out for this unique mode of transport. It would be a good day with two other cruise ships also anchored nearby, waiting to discharge their passengers.

But Kelsey barely registered the vista. All she could think about was the stunning turn of events *initiated by Ari*. It was all anyone could think about really. Certainly all they could talk about between themselves as they went about their work.

Luzviminda had insisted it was Ari – *Ari George*, she'd said over and over as her friends had hugged her tight earlier – who had been her advocate. Given how upset he'd been about the disparity of treatment a few nights ago, Kelsey wasn't surprised that Ari would do something like this, but still... who'd have thought one of the more rusted on members of the ship's staff could be out on his ear so damn quickly?

'You know what this means, don't you?' Tiffany said as they ate lunch together in the staff dining room.

Yup. Kelsey nodded. First opportunity she got, she was going to give that man a blow job. Okay, yes, they were done, and yes, she needed to stay the hell away from him, but a deed as good as this could not go unrewarded.

'They might start taking all complaints seriously now. Even against the officers. A pity your Ari wasn't on the boat when Jamilla was being dicked around.'

Your Ari. Those two words slid like a serpent through the dark recesses of Kelsey's mind. 'He's not my Ari.'

It was important to remember that.

To say out loud. Important that she *knew* it. After how he'd intervened on Luzviminda's behalf overnight, she was likely to start donning rose-coloured glasses and forget they were nothing more than a seriously fucked up indiscretion.

'Well, he should be. The man stood up for a *waitress*. Someone he didn't know. He's one of us, Kels.'

Kelsey smiled – Tiffany was giving her whiplash. 'I thought he was a bad idea?' she teased.

'Oh yeah.' She nodded. 'He's most definitely a bad idea. But it's too late now. Despite your insistence to the contrary, your emotions are already involved. At least you chose a good guy to crush your heart this time instead of a smarmy little con artist.'

One of the things Kelsey loved about Tiffany was that she didn't pull her punches. But sometimes, she wished her friend would deliver them with less of a jab. She *had* been a blind, naive, hopeless fool with Eric.

Not any more.

She'd learned her lesson. Inoculated herself against men – the good ones as well as the smarmy ones.

'No one's heart is getting crushed,' Kelsey said firmly.

Tiffany looked as if she was going to argue but rolled her eyes instead. 'Fine. At least promise me you're going to thank him for what he did.'

Kelsey laughed. 'I'm going to thank the pants right off that man.'

Tiffany grinned. 'That's my girl.'

8

Kelsey's chance at a special thank you came the next day after breakfast was over. She was clearing tables when Tiffany sidled up to her, taking the plates out of her hands.

'According to that cute new Peruvian waiter...'

Kelsey rolled her eyes. 'Ernesto.'

'Yes.' Tiffany nodded. 'Ernesto. Anyway, Ari is apparently spending the morning in his cabin working on some last-minute report his boss wants.'

Kelsey frowned. Ari's boss had ordered him to take leave and now he was bugging him with work? That hardly seemed fair.

'Go now. You won't be missed too much and we'll cover for you. You've got thirty minutes.'

Kelsey's belly pulled tight at the implication. Go have some kind of quickie, clandestine tryst in Ari's cabin in the middle of the day? In broad daylight. It was wildly inappropriate. Fraught with things that could go wrong and their resultant dire consequences.

But also secretly thrilling.

She didn't want to want Ari, but she did and she'd been hot for him ever since she'd found out what he'd done for Luzviminda. Hell, who was she kidding; she'd been hot for him since she met him but her motor had been revving like crazy this morning.

She'd *never* done anything so utterly daring.

Tiffany bugged her eyes at Kelsey. 'If you don't blow him, I will.'

Kelsey grinned. 'Time me.'

Pausing only to grab a tray out of the kitchen with an empty teapot and a teacup, Kelsey scurried to deck seven. Her heart was beating like a kettle drum with every step that took her closer, the sharp edges of anticipation prickling through her veins, tightening her nipples, tingling between her legs.

She was excruciatingly aware of the cameras in the passageways watching her every move. Excruciatingly aware as she smiled a polite hello at an elderly couple stepping out opposite Ari's cabin that not all passengers had decided to spend the day in Santorini.

Knocking on the door, her hand shaking, she said, 'Room service.'

Seconds later the door was opening and Ari was standing there, looking at her. 'I didn't order tea,' he murmured, his voice low, his gaze roving over her mouth and dropping to her neck and her cleavage, and Kelsey lost her breath for a beat or two.

'This isn't tea.'

She didn't wait for an invitation, she just shoved the tray at him and stepped straight into the room.

He chuckled as she advanced, stepping back and back and back until they were at the foot of the bed. 'What is it then?' he asked.

Kelsey smiled. 'It's thank you.'

She took the tray out of his hands and shoved it on the table, barely registering the papers strewn there and the open laptop. Then, she stepped in close, wound her arms around his neck and kissed him, long and deep and sloppy, filling her head with maple syrup and toothpaste. He groaned and slid his hands to her ass, pulling her in close, and for a moment Kelsey let the kiss run, let herself get lost. But, time was ticking.

Reluctantly, she pulled away.

'What was that for?'

His mouth was wet and a thrill zipped up her spine from base to nape. 'For Luzviminda.'

'Oh...' His dark gaze went a little wary. 'You heard about that?'

Kelsey laughed. 'Are you kidding? It's all over the staff quarters this morning. You're a goddamn hero.'

He shook his head. 'It wasn't anything.'

'Yes, it was. I think Tiffany wants to cast you in iron and mount you on the bow as a figurehead.'

He threw back his head and laughed, exposing the salt and pepper of scratchy whiskers, and Kelsey wanted to lick him there.

'Is she okay? Luzviminda? She assured me she was earlier this morning when we spoke but I don't think she is.'

Kelsey nodded. 'She's still a little shaken but they gave her the day off. I think the fact the sleazebucket's been removed from the ship has helped.'

'Has that happened before? With Jean Paul.'

She shrugged. 'He's always been... handsy, I guess. The kind of guy who stands a little too close, who accidentally brushes your body as he's passing, who stares a little too much, who makes sly sexual digs, you know? He tries it on with a lot of the newbies at least once but if you make a stand with him, he backs down.'

A vein pulsed in Ari's temple. 'Has he tried it with you?'

'No.' She shook her head. 'I think he prefers easier targets.'

'And nobody's ever complained?'

'Sure they have. But then they're either reassigned or transferred to another ship. He's good mates with a lot of the officers. Sometimes it's just better to deal with it yourself.'

'That's terrible,' Ari spluttered.

'Yeah.' Kelsey nodded. 'It is.' And it was. But it wasn't the first incident of questionable male behaviour on the face of the planet and unfortunately it wouldn't be the last. It could be pretty damn fraught being a woman. 'And then you came along,' she said, tightening her arms around his neck, 'and gave us all a little bit of hope.'

Ari rolled his eyes. 'I spoke up, that's all.'

'Well, whatever you said to HR it must have been something else because I've never known them to act so damn fast.'

Ari shook his head. 'I complained to the captain.'

Kelsey blinked. 'You did?'

'Of course I did.' He looked at her like that was the most logical course of action. 'I was making a serious allegation against a member of the crew. That kind of thing needs to go straight to the top. Jean Paul is damn lucky I couldn't persuade Luzviminda to report it to the police or they'd have been waiting for him when we docked.'

'Wow.' She smiled at him. 'You're kind of hot when you're kicking ass.'

Ari chuckled. 'It was the right thing to do.'

'Still…' She leaned in and kissed his neck, and she loved that his eyes fluttered closed. 'You're my hero.'

His amused-sounding 'Oh really?' buzzed against her lips as she brushed them against the thick thud of his pulse just to the left of his windpipe.

'Uh huh…' Her lips drifted lower. 'You wanna know what heroes get?'

'Capes?'

Kelsey laughed as she pulled away slightly, planting her hand in the centre of his chest and shoving, watching him land on his ass on the mattress behind. 'Blow jobs.'

A strangled kind of noise came from the back of his throat, which managed to be both endearing and hot as fuck. He reached for her, circling his arms around the backs of her thighs and pulling her in close. 'I don't need a sexual favour for being a decent human being, Kelsey.'

'I know,' she said, pushing on his shoulders to loosen his arms so she could kneel between his thighs.

His hand grabbed hers as she fingered the tab of his zipper, his hot dark gaze meeting hers and holding. 'I mean it. You don't need to… reward me.'

Integrity blazed in the inky depths, and hell if that wasn't the biggest turn on of all. 'I *know*.' She smiled, her green eyes dancing. 'But I want to.' Her fingers yanked down his fly. 'Now lay back and take your reward like a man.'

***

With the cries of Ari's orgasm quietening to loud pants, Kelsey pushed to her feet, backing away from the tempting bracket of his thighs. She straightened her skirt and blouse, the fabric skimming across her erect nipples, heightening her arousal. Her knees wobbled slightly both from the position she'd been in and the way he looked right now.

Mostly the way he looked right now.

He was fully clothed, and his spent cock – still impressively aroused – was the only part of him exposed. His arms were spread wide, his eyes were shut and his facial expression was somewhere between blissed-out and utterly trashed.

And *she'd* done that to him.

'Mmm,' she murmured, taking this opportunity to explore him fully, wishing she'd had the time to strip him naked. Wishing she had more time to spend, because climbing on top right now and seeing what he had left in the tank was mighty tempting. 'You look pretty damn rewarded to me.'

He cracked an eyelid open, then two, his gaze molten. 'Come here.' He lifted his arms with what seemed like a monumental effort on his behalf.

'Nope.' She shook her head. 'Gotta get back.'

He made grabby hands. 'I'll make it worth your while.'

Kelsey had zero doubt. The man had powers. 'I'm very busy, you know,' she said, a smile playing on her mouth.

He dropped his hands but his gaze sharpened then intensified as it drifted south, running over her body. The slick heat between her legs fired up and dampened her panties as he slowly found her eyes again.

'Fine, stay there,' he said, his voice a low rumble. 'Just take off your clothes.'

His low, silky suggestion slammed into her pelvis with all the power of a force ten gale. Kelsey was surprised the impact of it hadn't just torn the underwear from her body. It had certainly made her wetter. 'I'm going now.'

'Come back tonight.'

God, he was like Adam waving the apple at her. 'Ari...' Her voice held a note of warning and regret. They weren't supposed to be doing this. Sure, she'd come to his cabin and blown him, but there were extenuating circumstances.

He vaulted upright and Kelsey's breath caught. He should look silly with his dick out but he didn't. He was a prime male animal and the pheromones he was exuding enveloped her in a fog of lust.

'You gotta give me right of reply,' he said, his voice a low burr against her already aroused flesh.

'Ari... This has to stop.'

His eyes went suddenly hooded and she saw the kind of struggle there that was currently squalling around her insides. 'I know. I just didn't expect to want you so much.'

'Yeah.' Kelsey nodded, her eyes locking with his. 'Me neither.'

It didn't make her feel better and she probably shouldn't have admitted it to him, but it was the truth, damn it. And if he was man enough to own it then she was sure as hell woman enough.

'So come back tonight, after your shift. What time do you finish?'

'Eleven.' God, was that her voice? She sounded like she'd just smoked an entire packet of cigarettes.

'Okay. Good. Come back here after and let me...' His gaze drifted down her body and zeroed in on the juncture of her thighs, and Kelsey was surprised her skirt didn't burst into flames. He flicked his gaze back to her face. 'Repay the favour.'

Kelsey felt the low pull of his words deep inside her sex, the muscles clenching in anticipation. She should say no.

But the man *was* a freak with his tongue.

'I... don't know,' she obfuscated. 'Maybe.'

What she was doing was against the rules. She could lose her job. Fall short of her goals after seven hard years of being away from home and family, working long shifts and having zero privacy, all so she could provide a comfortable and dignified life for her mother.

She'd already been stupid where one man was concerned – had she learned nothing? But there was just something about Ari George that made her want to throw caution to the wind.

'What does that mean?' he asked.

Good question. Kelsey hated that a guy she hadn't even known four days ago could have her in such a dither. Sexual frustration and denial were like prickles under her skin, needling and irritating. 'It means maybe,' she said, testily.

'Okay.' He held up his hands in a placatory manner.

His calmness added more prickles. 'I really have to go.'

'Then go.'

His voice wasn't angry or accusatory or sulky. It was completely without emotion or emphasis. But, given what had just happened between them, his absence of emotion increased the prickle count exponentially.

God*damn* it. She *did not* want to go. But she did. She turned around, grabbed the tray and exited his cabin.

* * *

Kelsey didn't go to Ari after her shift. With Jean Paul gone there was controlled chaos all day as Ramon made a series of changes, and that night, when he asked her to work the casino bar after her shift at the Aphrodite Lounge finished, she'd said yes.

She could have said no but the bar staff at the casino earned the best tips. And as tempting as Ari's proposition was, it was important to remember she'd been working on cruise ships for seven years for the *money*, not sexy Greek men.

In a nine-month contract, she could earn about thirty thousand Aussie dollars and, with the tip money on top and no outgoing expenses, she was able to save almost all her income.

She *had* to remember her long-term financial goals.

Remember the cottage in Pelican Bay she wanted so much for her and her mother, who was going to be fully dependant in the next few years. Ari was for a week – her mother was for life.

So she worked the casino bar and hung with her bestie all night and between the two of them, the punters were kept charmed, liquored up and very happy to part with generous tips. And she refused to wonder what Ari was thinking about her absence or to feel guilty. She'd made him no promises.

But she was out on her feet at quarter after five the following morning when she and Tiff finally headed back to their cabins. Through the portholes, Kelsey could see they were docking in the port of Pireaus and she knew, in a few hours, passengers would be disembarking to spend the day in Athens.

But *she* would be snatching a few hours' sleep because she had to be back on again in five hours for a ten-hour shift. It wouldn't be anywhere near enough after pulling an all-nighter, but Ramon had offered her tomorrow off as recompense, so it was worth it. She'd finish at ten tonight and wouldn't have to be back at work until 6 p.m. the following evening.

She could sleep then. In fact, she planned to. She was going to sleep every last minute of it.

* * *

Unfortunately, at 11 p.m., Kelsey was still wide awake. She was tired, *so tired*, but her mind was ticking over. Thinking about Ari. Thinking about how they'd left it yesterday morning.

She'd seen him in the restaurant tonight and he'd smiled and nodded politely, making the briefest of eye contact. The sort of interaction he had with any of the servers, and that had felt... like a blow to her ribs.

It was ridiculous. It was *exactly* how she wanted him to treat her – like she was just another woman on the ship. One he hadn't seen naked. But the lack of acknowledgement had... hurt.

Freaking hell. What was wrong with her?

Kelsey rolled onto her side and pulled the covers over her head, ordering herself to stop. Stop thinking about him. Stop remembering how good they were between the sheets. Stop remembering the timbre of his voice or the way he slipped into Greek in the throes of pleasure.

But God, she wanted to hear him in the throes of pleasure again. Although she'd settle for just hearing his voice, period.

And she owed him an apology, right? For the weird way it had ended yesterday morning.

Right.

Decision made, Kelsey rolled up into a sitting position and reached across for the cabin phone. Before she could talk herself out of it, she direct dialled his cabin, lying down on her side again, pulling the covers back over her head.

Lordy. What was she doing? Her pulse pounded so loudly through her ears she was amazed she even heard him pick up.

'Hello?'

Kelsey shut her eyes on a hot flood of relief. *Man...* he sounded good. Soft and low and sleepy as the silence on the line stretched between them, and Kelsey, who was having a sudden attack of the doubts, almost hung up. It was only his rumbly 'Kelsey?' that stopped her.

Gripping the phone, she pressed her lips together for a moment, her pulse roaring through her ears. 'I'm sorry,' she said, her voice husky. 'About yesterday morning. About being a little... testy.'

There was a pause for a beat or two then a gruff, 'It's okay.'

'I...' Kelsey swallowed. In the dark, with her crazy-mixed-up feelings for him stirring around inside her, it seemed easy to confess. 'I want you too much, Ari.'

'*Theé mou...* Kelsey.' He groaned her name like it was some kind of endearment, and he'd never sounded more damn Greek. 'The things you do to me.'

His words stroked between her legs and wrapped around her heart. 'I shouldn't have called,' she whispered. Even down a phone line she wanted him.

'Come to me.' His voice was rough as gravel. 'Please...'

Kelsey shut her eyes at his husky request so full of need it oozed into every part of her body. She squeezed the phone hard and her thighs even harder. *Ugh.* Why couldn't she just say *no* to him? Hang up the damn phone. Why was it so difficult to turn her back on him, to draw a line?

Not doing so was playing with fire.

Logically, she knew that. Logically, she knew she held the power to extinguish it. But Kelsey wasn't operating on logic where Ari was concerned.

She was being led by something much less rational.

'*Kelsey*... I can't think for wanting you.'

Oh God. She knew exactly how he felt. She couldn't process anything but the need for him coursing through her veins.

'This is madness,' she whispered.

'I know.'

Sighing into the phone, she murmured, 'I'm coming.' And then she hung up.

Driven by an imperative she didn't understand, but wasn't about to ignore, Kelsey leapt out of bed and threw on some clothes – yoga pants and a T-shirt. Scraping her hair into a messy knot, she zipped up a hoodie, pushed her feet into flip-flops and shoved some Ōceanós-issued condoms into the front hoodie pocket.

Ten minutes later, grateful for the head covering to obscure her identity, she was at Ari's door. It opened on the first knock and she barely had time to register that he was in nothing but his underwear before he was dragging her inside, pulling her into his arms, pushing her against the closing door and kissing her.

Kissing her hard. Kissing her deep. Kissing her long. Giving her the rough pant of his breath and the deep resonance of his groans and the wicked stroke of his tongue. Sweeping into her mouth, plundering every quarter of hers until she was moaning and sighing and clinging and grinding against the hardness inside his underwear.

He pulled away abruptly and they stared at each other for long moments. Kelsey's heart raced and their combined breathing sounded like a hurricane. Slowly, he released her, a smile on his mouth as his hands dropped from her hips and he backed up. And he backed up some more, then some more.

The smile on his lips grew bigger and Kelsey was too flummoxed by the kiss to do anything much at the moment other than watch. He stopped when his calves hit the mattress and he lowered his ass to the bed, his gaze intense as it dropped from her face and drifted south to touch every part of her body.

Slickness built between her legs as he slowly found her eyes again. He crooked his finger. 'Come here.'

Kelsey could no more have disobeyed that imperious finger than flown to the moon. She walked towards him on shaky legs, the thick bound of her abdominal pulse a hot throb in her belly.

'Now, where were we?' he asked, his voice soft as he leaned back onto his elbows, his gaze taking another slow turn of her body before returning to her face. 'Oh yes... that's right. Take off your clothes.'

Her hands trembling a little, Kelsey withdrew the strip of three condoms from the hoodie pocket and tossed them at Ari. He caught them in a move that looked pure reflex and, grunting his approval, tossed them on the bed.

She unzipped then, removing the hoodie as she kicked out of her flip-flops. The T-shirt came next. She wasn't wearing a bra and the harsh suck of his breath as her breasts tumbled free had her nipples hardening to tight achy points. Shimmying her hips, she pushed off the yoga pants, leaving her in nothing but a black lace bikini brief.

He didn't say anything, just let his gaze wander over every inch of her body. Kelsey pointed to his underwear. 'Your turn,' she said, her voice thick.

He shook his head and pointed at the scrap of lace hindering his view. His gaze was so intent on the space between her legs it felt as if that finger was actually stroking her there.

'Those first.' His voice had dropped so low it wasn't much more than a disturbance of the air.

Sliding her thumbs beneath the fabric bracketing each hip, she pulled them down, shimmying once again as the black lace slipped down her legs. She kicked them and the yoga pants aside with a brief sweep of her foot.

She was totally naked now and not remotely self-conscious as he stared at her like she was the best damn piece of Baklava he'd ever seen. His nostrils flared. 'Come here.'

Kelsey shook her head, glancing at his underwear. 'Now you.'

Without taking his eyes off her face, Ari stood and divested himself of the last barrier. His height and breadth suddenly dominated the room as he stood gloriously, arrogantly naked, his cock springing free, jutting from his body.

It was so fucking potent it made her dizzy.

Sitting again, his stiff cock rising like a trident between his legs, he reached for a condom. Still not taking his eyes off her, he ripped the foil open. Kelsey's heart beat a little faster as she watched his deft fingers fit the thin latex protection over his cock.

Her breath got caught somewhere in her throat as he worked it all the way down his magnificent girth. It was an enthralling show.

'Kelsey.' His voice was rough as tree bark and she dragged her gaze away from the weapon primed and loaded in his lap. He crooked his finger again. 'Come here.'

She didn't refuse this time. She practically ran the four paces to where he was sitting and stepped right into the space between his legs, her hands sliding onto his warm shoulders.

His palms settled on the backs of her thighs, just above her knees, and her skin hummed at his touch.

'*Eísai ómorfi,*' he whispered.

She had no idea what he'd said but she didn't need a translation; it was there in his eyes. His head was level with her chest and he was looking at her breasts, with a reverence in his expression that was both heart- *and* panty-melting.

His fingers slowly stroked their way up to her ass and Kelsey almost whimpered at the havoc they were creating. After long moments, he pressed his forehead to her sternum, burying his face in her cleavage. He inhaled then, roughly. Once, twice, three times, before turning his face and planting a kiss on the slope of her left breast.

It was the lightest of touches, barely there, yet Kelsey felt it all the way to her clit. The screamingly hard nub between her legs throbbed at the stimulus and she swayed a little as she drew in a ragged breath.

His hands gripped the back of her thighs and Kelsey sunk her fingers into the hair at his nape. Whether she was gaining purchase or just wanted to keep him there, she didn't know, she just knew it felt more than sexual to hold him close.

He turned his face and pressed a kiss to the other slope before giving his lips and tongue full reign, exploring every millimetre of her breasts. Licking and kissing, drawing wet patterns until he reached her nipples, sucking each one into the hot recess of his mouth.

Kelsey cried out, burying her hands deeper into his hair and arching her back as he switched from side to side until she was a giant quivering mass of nonsensical noises. Until her legs were weak and she was floating in a sea of pleasure – the smell of maple syrup and her own arousal thick in her nostrils.

And just when Kelsey thought she couldn't take any more, that the low pull in her abdomen was sure to swell into something bigger and harder and that she was actually going to orgasm from nipple stimulation, his fingers went exploring.

She gasped as they burrowed between her legs, stroking the plump, slick seam of her sex with absolute precision. The pleasure cranked from intoxicating to almost vicious in its intensity, her knees buckling under its onslaught.

Ari's thighs clamped firm around her, keeping her upright, keeping her in place as his fingers prodded for entry. Kelsey cried out as first one finger, then another, found their way deep inside her, the walls of her sex contracting tight at the thick, blunt intrusion.

'You're so wet,' he muttered around her nipple before scraping his teeth against the hard aroused point and sliding another finger to the swollen knot of nerves at the apex of her slippery inner folds.

It was all it took, just a few rubs of her clit and the low pull morphed into an intense ball of pleasure uncoiling in one almighty release, streaking rapture like lightning to every cell in her body.

Kelsey's breath strangled in her lungs as she called his name. '*Ari!*'

Her body bucked as the sensation unfurled with flashpoint intensity, breaking like a storm, and he groaned as the hot, wet channel of her pussy clamped tight around his fingers.

Kelsey didn't know how long it lasted. She lost all sense of time as wave after wave rocked her and spun her around. All she knew was her heart was still hammering and her clit was still quivering, and she'd barely regained the strength in her legs when Ari slid his fingers from her body.

'*Theé*, Kelsey.' He dropped fevered kisses all over her chest, her neck, her collarbones and breasts. '*Se chreiázomai kai theló na se gamiso.*'

She didn't understand the Greek but his hands felt good sliding over her body, saturated as it was with sensation. His touch showered sparks up and down her legs as he urged them apart, and hot whispers straight into her ear in his mother tongue fanned goosebumps down her neck.

The low timbre of his voice washed over her dreamily as her knees widened and she lowered into his lap, her big toes just touching the floor. The thick, hard nudge of him against the slick lips of her sex finally brought her back to herself. She moaned and opened her eyes, finding him watching her, his mouth a straight line, his jaw rigid, his eyes dark and intense.

'*Agápi mou.*' His chest heaved. 'I need you.'

The combination of his soft endearment and his expression of quiet desperation undid her, and Kelsey kissed him, long and deep, feeling between them for his latex-covered shaft and notching him at her entrance.

9

Ari fell back, groaning as she slowly swallowed him up, her moan of satisfaction lighting a fire in his belly as his fingers closed convulsively around her hips. She fell forward, gasping 'So good' as she took him all the way to the hilt, her forehead pressing to his chest.

Then she raised herself up, anchoring her hands on his shoulders and leaning all her weight forward, her jaw set, her gaze locking on his like a heat-seeking missile. Raising a hand to her hair, she pulled it out of its knot and sent it cascading around her shoulders.

'Don't move,' she whispered. 'Let me.'

The instruction went straight to his balls and Ari's hands tightened on her hips as he let her take control. She rocked against him then, a glaze in her eyes that told Ari all he was going to need to do was to hang on. And hang on he did as she set up a rhythm, her full breasts swaying hypnotically to the rock of her hips.

Her tightness undulated along his shaft in an erotic grip that ratcheted up his heart rate and squeezed the muscles of his thighs and ass and belly in a vice. But it clearly wasn't enough for Kelsey, a frustrated grimace marring her features as she leaned forward, leaned into the hands that were gripping his shoulders.

But still it didn't seem enough as she half growled, half whimpered, shutting her eyes and sinking her teeth into the cupid's bow of her top lip, her hair forming a curtain around her face.

She was *magnificent*. Like an avenging angel hunting down an orgasm it seemed she couldn't quite reach.

She stole Ari's breath.

He slid his hand from her hip to the slick heat between her legs. 'No,' she said, panting as her hips flexed faster. 'Too sensitive.'

'Tell me.' He withdrew his hand. 'Tell me what you need.'

Anything. He'd do anything.

An aggravated little mewling noise slipped from her lips as her eyes blinked open and zeroed in on his. 'I don't know,' she said, her tone desperate as one of her hands turned from gripping his shoulder to pummelling it a couple of times. 'It's... just... there.'

Her arms trembled and her thighs trembled, and her face was flushed and he could see the mad flutter of her pulse at the base of her throat. Air chugged in and out of her lungs in breathy gasps.

'What about this?'

He thrust then as she sank down and she cried out, her green eyes widening, her fingernails sinking into the flesh of his shoulders. 'Oh God.' She moaned and her eyes almost rolled back in her head. 'Yes.'

Her guttural approval was like petrol to the flame burning in his loins and Ari thrust again, harder this time.

She gasped as her head rocked. 'Yes. Just like that.'

Grunting as he leashed the relentless pull of his own orgasm, Ari gave it to her again, *just like that*.

'Please, yes...' Kelsey bore down harder through her arms, moaning loud. 'Don't stop.'

Stop? He *never* wanted to stop.

Ari slammed his cock into her, revelling in the tight sheath of her pussy. Three more thrusts and Kelsey's eyes flew open, her lips parting on a gasp that ricocheted around the cabin. She cried out then, the sexiest damn banshee noise he'd ever heard.

'Yesss!'

Her entire body tightened, her fingernails sunk into the flesh of his shoulders, her back arched. Their gazes held as she ground against him, her pussy fisting his cock, squeezing hard as her body trembled and shook to the pulse of her orgasm, her wild moans a powerful aphrodisiac.

He joined her, the orgasm he'd been holding back breaking like a dam. Their climaxes intertwined, the rhythmic squeeze of her pussy and the hot pulse of his cock locking them together as Ari spilled inside her until they were both spent and he collapsed onto the mattress, pulling her down on top of him.

'*Theé dóse mou dýnami*,' Ari said eventually as he stirred beneath her, his hands sifting through the fan of her hair. 'We're good at this.'

She laughed but it sounded heavy and sleepy. 'I think *phenomenal* is more accurate.'

Her warm breath was like a lightning rod against his skin, goosebumps erupting across his scalp and prickling down his nape. She was right; their chemistry was phenomenal.

Propping her chin on his chest, she traced his bottom lip with her finger. The sensation slid all the way down to pool in his groin. 'I missed you,' she murmured, her voice sounding sleepy, and before he could respond, she laid her cheek on his chest again and he heard her yawn.

Ari's heart thunked in his chest. He'd missed her too. He'd known her for only a handful of days but it was the truth.

When he'd told her to go yesterday, it hadn't been churlish. He hadn't been angry or annoyed. He understood the risk Kelsey was taking and that pushing her to stay had been wrong. Not to mention unethical on his part. He was supposed to be working undercover investigating the ship's failings, not putting Kelsey in a compromising situation all whilst deceiving her about his actual identity.

It'd been the wakeup call he needed, a resetting of *his* boundaries.

But her voice on the phone had reached inside him and swept them all away as he'd *throbbed* with the need to see her one more time. Being like this with another woman hadn't been on his radar. Hell, it hadn't even been on his wish list, and that was confusing and confrontational, but he *wanted* Kelsey and she wanted him.

And the world *hadn't* ended. He hadn't fallen apart.

Ari didn't think for a moment he'd been *cured* of grief – he still wasn't ready to let go of Talia – but maybe he was finally emerging into the light?

Thanks to Kelsey.

'I missed you too,' he said, but she was already asleep.

* * *

Kelsey woke the next morning to the trail of fingers at her hip, a warm solid body spooning her from behind and a seriously large erection making itself felt in the cleft of her butt cheeks.

'Mmmm.' She stretched a little but didn't open her eyes, just luxuriated in the feel of Ari and the certainty that she didn't have to go anywhere today. She snuggled into the cradle of his thighs and the virile length of his cock.

'*Kalimera.*'

The greeting rumbled around her, low and sexy, as Ari dropped a kiss on her shoulder. Kelsey had heard Ari curse, come and mutter dirty words in his native tongue, but there was something nice about his innocent morning greeting, and the way it slid out, all rough and sleepy, caused a glow deep inside her chest.

His hand moved steadily north to her ribs and she smiled. 'Good morning to you too.'

Lips buzzed their way across her shoulder blade to the bony notch where nape met spine and Kelsey wriggled against his dick suggestively. 'What time is it?'

The cabin was as dark as ever but she could hear the distant shutting of doors and the muffled chatter of people as they walked past the cabin, so it had to be morning.

'Eight thirty.'

Kelsey's eyes flashed open. 'Really?' She hadn't slept this late since her last stint home between contracts.

Not that there'd been a lot of sleeping going on.

'Uh huh.' A hot tongue swiped up the side of her neck as his fingers traced the ruts of her ribs. 'We wore each other out.'

'Mmm.' She sighed as she shut her eyes again. They *had* fucked like demons after she'd taken a little nap. But his body didn't seem *that* worn out. Nor was hers if the heat smouldering between her legs was any indicator.

'Doesn't feel like it.' She ground against him, her heart skipping a beat or two as his breath caught. The smoulder flickered to flame. 'We should do something about that.'

Ari had been delighted to hear about her day off and had suggested they spend it in his cabin. Kelsey knew she shouldn't be encouraging whatever the hell this was. Prior to meeting Ari, her rule had been to never stay the night with a guy – to do the deed and leave. But she'd now stayed with him *twice*.

And was going to spend the day with him, too.

She was stepping over lots of lines here. Pushing boundaries. Work related and personal. And, for someone as goal orientated and disciplined as Kelsey, that was big. But in a few days, she'd never see him again and she just didn't have the willpower to deny herself the sex *or* the snuggles any more.

It seemed to her that he'd given up trying to deny it too.

'I've been thinking,' he said, his teeth grazing the spot where her pulse beat unsteadily in her throat, his fingers stroking the underside of her breast.

Her nipple burgeoned at the touch. 'Oh?'

'Come into Mykonos with me.'

Kelsey's eyes blinked open. Okay... that she hadn't been expecting. She remembered he'd expressed an interest in only seeing Mykonos, so she supposed it shouldn't be surprising he wanted to go. This was his holiday after all. But...

'I can't. I can't be seen with you even off the ship.'

Not to mention it felt like another boundary she was pushing. Surrendering to this crazy impulse on the ship was one thing. Something in her blissed-out state she was just managing to justify. Taking this thing to a second location?

That felt like something more than a cruise ship fling.

His whiskers spiked against her shoulder blade as he anchored his chin there. 'I know. I'm not talking about walking the streets together. My boss owns a house on Mykonos. He said I could use it when the ship docked for the day if I wanted. You should see it, Kelsey, it's beautiful with this infinity edge pool that looks out over the sea. You can join me there and no one need know. Just you and me skinny dipping and—'

His hand finally quit teasing around her breast and slid over the top. Kelsey shivered and her belly pulled tight.

'Making out.' His thumb teased her nipple. 'Plus, the housekeeper there makes the best spanakopita.'

Kelsey's eyes shut as his fingers strummed at her nipple, sparking sensation to all her erogenous zones, blowing away all her very sensible reasons for staying on board. They floated away like dandelion puffs in her mind's eye as the lure of spending a day away from the ship with Ari beckoned.

No hiding, no sneaking around. Just... normal. It didn't have to mean it was something more, right?

'Well... I do like to eat,' she said, surrendering to the temptation, her voice raspy as his fingers grew rougher with her nipple.

'So do I.'

Kelsey snaked her arm up and behind her, anchoring it around his neck as she arched into the palm of his hand. 'I'm not talking about food.' Right now she was only hungry for his dick.

'Neither am I.'

* * *

Ari stood on the terrace squinting against the vicious sparkle of morning sun on the calm blue of what was now the Aegean. It was blindingly blue. As blindingly blue as the building behind was blindingly white and the bougainvillea creeping over the facade was blindingly purple.

It was all blindingly fucking perfect.

Not even the large white monolith of their cruise ship at anchor, blindingly modern in this ancient vista, spoiled the beauty.

It had been too long since he'd been here and he'd forgotten how it called to him. How the island and the water spoke to him. How it had soothed his soul and nurtured him through his darkest hours.

It was actually Theo's house but Ari had holed up here after Talia's death. Choosing here, choosing Mykonos, had been easy. Talia had never been to the island, to the house. They'd talked about it many times but things had always cropped up and it had never eventuated. Fortuitous, as it turned out, because Ari had been able to exist here without memories confronting him at every turn.

He'd done that for a year. A year until Theo's patience with Ari's isolation had worn thin and he'd dragged his brother back to Athens, back to the bosom of the family, and put him to work.

And now he was bringing a woman here. A woman other than his wife. He took a moment to reflect on what a huge step that was. So big, he almost hadn't taken it. Had fought the words on the tip of his tongue, his mind grappling with the warring elements of insane need for Kelsey and guilt about letting someone into his life.

But even through the disquiet, it hadn't felt *wrong*. It still didn't. Which was confusing because surely it should?

Surely this feeling that it was *right* wasn't rational?

God... Ari didn't know. All he knew was that he *wanted* to share Mykonos with Kelsey, and this push-pull he felt over whatever the hell it was they were doing was exhausting.

The faint tinkle of the doorbell broke into Ari's reverie and he hurried inside, determined to put all his doubt and angst away and just enjoy himself. It had been three long years since he'd enjoyed himself; surely he was allowed one day?

The cool mosaic tiles were a relief to his bare feet as he strode past whitewashed walls to the front door, anticipation quickening his step. He felt stupidly breathless as he pulled it open to find Kelsey beaming at him in a halter neck sundress, her bikini straps on display, her face almost obscured by a big floppy hat and dark sunglasses.

'*Kalimera*,' she said in a light musical tone, offering him a paper umbrella, and Ari's lungs felt too big for his chest.

He took the umbrella with one hand and grabbed her around the waist with the other, tugging her close. She swept the hat off her head, her hair tumbling loose around her shoulders, and Ari kissed her deep and hungry as he kicked the door shut.

'C'mon,' he whispered, pulling himself away with difficulty, but if he didn't let her go he was going to drag her down to the tiles and they had all day to be uncivilised. 'Come see the terrace.'

Ari was not disappointed by Kelsey's reaction. 'Oh. My. God.'

Her head swept from side to side to take in the full one-eighty-degree view. Dumping her hat and bright orange tote bag on the mosaic-topped table, Kelsey made her way around the elegant curves of the swimming pool to the railing.

Wrapping her fingers around it, she sighed. 'This is... stunning.'

Ari came to a halt behind her, the front of his thighs aligning with the back of hers, his hands sliding onto her shoulders. Her head tucked in perfectly under his chin. She fit against him just right. *They* fit just right.

'You like?'

'It's beautiful.' She relaxed into his frame. 'How amazing would it be to actually live here?'

'You'd like that?'

Her hair tickled his throat as she nodded. 'Hell yeah. Who wouldn't? This is my dream.'

'To live here?' he teased.

'No. Well... yes,' she said with a self-deprecating laugh. 'I'm a realist though, so I'll settle for this cottage in a little seaside town a few hours north of where I live. It's not much more than a shack really and the roof leaks, but Mum and I go there every holiday and we love it. Waking up to the sound of waves on the beach, seeing the ocean through the windows...'

She sighed and the wistful note in her voice wrapped fingers around Ari's heart.

'That's my dream. A sea change. That's why I've been cruising for seven years, saving all my money.'

'It sounds nice.'

'It is.' She gave another deprecating laugh. 'My mother says I must have been a mermaid in a previous life. I think she might be right.'

'Oh, really?' Ari reached for the knot of her halter neck and pulled it loose. 'Care to get in the pool and prove it?'

Her dress slid down to her waist to reveal two plain black triangles straining to hold her breasts in place. Ari's breath hitched. *Póso panémorfa.* She had gorgeous tits. He reached for the knot of her bikini top next.

'I need to be topless to prove I'm a mermaid?'

She was obviously amused but just as obviously turned on, a fact he could hardly miss from his vantage point as the two tight points of her nipples tented the triangles of fabric.

'Mermaids don't wear bikinis.'

'Ariel does.'

He smiled. 'Ariel wears shells.'

As he pulled on the bow at her nape, the straps slipped from his fingers and the triangles peeled away from the ripe mounds of her breasts. Her nipples stood taut and proud and Ari groaned at the sight.

'*Eísai san theá*,' he muttered, trekking his lips down her neck as his hands slid around and cupped her breasts.

She moaned and arched as his fingers brushed her nipples and Ari's cock went as hard as the whitewashed stone of the house.

'Anyone can see us,' she said on a half gasp.

It was true, there were houses all around, both beside and behind, jutting out to make the most of the views. And the people in those houses *could*, if they were so inclined, see him fondling her breasts. But Ari was in thrall.

He wasn't generally an exhibitionist but he couldn't stop touching her, looking at her, stripped to the waist, her head thrown back, her nipples tipped golden beneath the glorious Greek sunshine.

'Nobody knows us,' he whispered. Which wasn't strictly true. Ari *did* know people on Mykonos. Or he *had*, anyway. And they'd all be working in the bars by now.

Still, she pulled away, slipping out from where his body had caged her against the railing, scooting behind him, leaving him a mass of jangling nerve endings. It was worth it, though, to find her naked but for her bikini bottoms when he turned.

Smiling at him, she pulled the hip ties simultaneously and the fabric fell away. His breath left his lungs on a hot hiss of air. She was gorgeous. Everything round and soft and perfect.

He'd spent a lot of the last few years convinced he was cursed by bad luck. But, right at this moment, he felt like his stars were changing.

'Well?' She shoved a hand on her hip and cocked an eyebrow. 'Are you joining me or not?'

Then she turned and dived into the pool.

A wet spray to his face revived him and it took Ari no time at all to shuck his clothes and dive into the clear, cool water. She was just about at the end as Ari struck out after her, the water cool as silk on his skin.

She was staring at the view, her forearms resting flat on the infinity edge, when he caught her up. Despite being in the deep end, he could still stand flat-footed and she sighed as he pressed all his hardness against her softness and licked at water droplets on her neck.

'God,' she whispered, 'this view.'

The view *was* incredible. The sapphire of the Aegean, the majestic lines of the *Hellenic Spirit*, the random, higgledy-piggledy placement of the whitewashed houses around them, the famous Mykonos windmills in the distance.

But nothing beat the sight of her. The ends of her wet hair dripping a trail of droplets down the slope of her breasts to the tips of her nipples. The line of her neck. The ridge of her collarbone.

Nothing beat the feel of her either. Her body was smooth and soft against his and the cool press of her ass cheeks against the rampant heat of his cock was seriously addictive.

'You like it.'

'Yes.'

Ari slid his hands to her breasts, kneading and squeezing. 'What about this?'

'Mmm,' she said on a low, breathy moan as she arched into his hands.

'And this.' One hand headed south, his fingers sliding between her legs. She wasn't cool there. She was hot. Hot and a different kind of wet. Slick and slippery.

Wet for him.

She gasped as he found her clitoris. 'God, yes.' Reaching behind her as she had this morning, she anchored her fingers in his hair. 'I like that a lot.'

Ari's heart pounded in his chest, the water almost vibrating around him in time to the beat. 'Spread your legs.'

He'd expected her to part them out sideways but she curled her legs up behind her – behind him – her heels grounding in the backs of his thighs, splaying herself wide and locking them together tight.

She gasped and he groaned as his finger slid into her tight, wet heat. '*Christe*,' he muttered, his voice as rough and heavy as the air chugging in and out of his lungs, his cock heavy, straining for action. He sunk another finger inside her, feeling her clamp tight around him.

'*Aaarrriii.*'

The way she moaned his name like that, all low and sonorous like he'd connected to something deep, something beyond physical, kicked him hard in the chest.

'What?' he whispered in her ear. 'Tell me what you want.'

'You. Inside me.'

His cock voted for that too but... 'No condom.' His thumb slid to the hard pearl of her clitoris, her body bucking against his as he teased lightly over the top. 'And I'm not getting out to get one.'

He wasn't leaving this position until she'd screamed his name so damn loud the gods heard her on Mount Olympus.

'I don't care,' she said, panting and bucking against him as he continued to tease her nipple, her clit *and* her g-spot.

Ari frowned. 'Don't care?' His fingers stilled.

This elicited a frustrated little growl at the back of her throat but, undeterred, she took over, seeking her own pleasure, riding his fingers as she fisted her hand in his hair.

'Don't care... about a condom.' Her breathing was laboured as she flexed her hips back and forth. 'I just need you in me. *Now.*'

Her guttural admission hit Ari right between the legs. His cock, jammed tight between the cleft of her buttocks, bucked, his ass contracted and his pulse pounded through his chest in anticipation.

Christe, he wanted that.

Wanted to feel her tight, wet heat surrounding him, wanted to feel every nuance of her orgasm as she came on him, milking his dick from root to tip.

'*Ari!*' She gasped his name with such frustrated impatience it was almost his undoing. 'I have a contraceptive implant, no diseases and I'm your first sexual partner in three years.'

A strangled little whimper gurgled from her mouth as she ground against his hand and her fingers clenched and unclenched in his hair. 'I think we're covered.'

Her voice was all high and breathy like she was almost there, like all he'd need to do was brush his thumb over her clit. Or slide his cock deep inside her – his taut, aching, *bare* cock.

'Please...'

Ari's heart slammed in his chest. He wanted to be inside her as badly as she needed him to be there and nothing, not even Zeus himself, could have stopped Ari from giving Kelsey what she wanted. What *he* wanted.

What they *needed*.

With her legs locking him in tight, there wasn't much room to manoeuvre, so he released her breast and slid his hand between their bodies. Grasping his cock, he angled it, ploughing it through the seam of her sex and notching himself at her entrance.

She bucked violently at the stimulus and moaned, 'Yessssss,' long and low.

And it was like a siren song in his blood, clamping a fist around his balls and shooting a flaming arrow right up the furrow of his spine as he anchored his hands on her hips, pushed through the balls of his feet and thrust. She cried out – a noise somehow sated *and* feral – and he grunted as she swallowed him up.

Gamoto.

She was tight and hot and wet and already quivering around him, and he felt in-*fucking*-vincible. Like Poseidon rising from the sea.

And also like he was... home.

Being locked together as they were didn't allow for a lot of thrusting, but she didn't need it, just the slightest flex of his pelvis pushed her over the edge. '*Yes.*' Kelsey's moans and pants filled his head. 'God, Ari... I'm coming.'

Yes, she was. Coming on his dick in long, urgent squeezes that plucked at the piano-wire tension of muscles buried deep at the root of his cock, her heels grinding like a drill bit into the backs of his thighs. He had to mentally recite the Greek tax laws to hold on to his load.

Finally she was spent, her heels unlocking, her legs returning to their natural position, her body heavy as her forehead slumped onto her arms still resting against the infinity edge of the pool. Her arms and his cock inside her were the only things stopping her from sliding boneless into the water.

'I'm sorry,' she said, lifting her head, 'I couldn't wait.'

Her head wobbled precariously like her neck was made out of marshmallow, and Ari slid his hand onto her throat, his thumb notching under the angle of her jaw for support. She swallowed and he felt the muscles undulate beneath his palm as surely as he felt the thick beat of her carotid against his fingers.

'It's okay,' he crooned quietly near her ear. 'Watch.' He nuzzled her earlobe. 'Watch the world while I fuck you.'

It was what it felt like right now, that they had the world at their feet. And he was a *God*.

Ari withdrew almost all the way out before thrusting all the way in again and it felt *so damn good*, her tight flesh massaging his length. It sucked his breath away. He did it again and Kelsey moaned, and her head rocked and Ari's fingers firmed around her throat for more support.

'Yes,' she panted. 'Yes.'

Ari withdrew and thrust again and she said, 'Beautiful. It's so beautiful, Ari.'

'No.' Ari shook his head as he picked up the rhythm, squashing her breasts against the side of the pool, the water swirling around them like a whirlpool. 'You're beautiful,' he muttered. 'You're a goddess.'

He thrust deeper – *harder* – as his orgasm rippled up from the root of his cock, hotter than the Mykonos sun. His fingers found her clit, flying over the top, making her buck, making her moan and cry out, 'Ari, Ari, *Ari*,' her throat moving convulsively as the tight, hot sheath of her gloved him, milking his climax straight out of his balls.

Diamonds of sunshine spilled around him. Diamonds in the sea and the air and the pool. Diamonds in her hair.

A kaleidoscope of pleasure as he joined her in the rapture.

10

Kelsey smiled as Ari swam up behind her, joining her at the infinity edge again. He fit around her perfectly and she revelled in all his solid, naked flesh.

She'd had the most divine few hours of her life. Swimming with Ari, chatting about Mykonos and laughing over his funny Greek stories. Eating olives and Dolmades and the most divine Spanakopita. Sipping a cool locally grown white wine as they lazed in the sunshine and *made out* in the pool.

She sighed, already sad that today was going to end. Ari dropped a kiss on her shoulder. 'She's magnificent, isn't she?'

Kelsey's gaze came back into focus and she realised she'd been staring at the *Hellenic Spirit*. 'Why are ships always chick names?'

'Ah, the age-old question.' Amusement laced his voice as his lips nuzzled back and forth between her neck and shoulder, his breath warm as it fanned over her skin, spreading prickles of awareness down to the hardening tips of her nipples. 'Some say it's because a ship is a vessel, like a woman is a vessel for a child.'

She shuddered. 'That's some kind of patriarchal bullshit.'

'Yes.' He laughed. 'I prefer the more poetic explanation.'

'And what's that?'

'The whimsy of men. Personifying objects of beauty with feminine characteristics.'

'Hmmm.' Kelsey wasn't sure that sounded much better, but her eyes hurt from the beauty all around her and she didn't want to ruin the mood. She wanted to soak up every nuance of this glorious day.

'Your boss must be rich,' she said as her eyes lazily followed the wake of a small boat, foaming white against the brilliant blue.

His lips lifted from where they'd been teasing. 'He's... not short of a quid.'

She sighed, remembering how comforting it had been when she'd thought she had money to burn. 'That must be nice.'

'To be rich?'

'Yeah.'

'You want to be rich?'

'No. Not really. I was rich, once... for a while, anyway. It didn't bring me much joy. I'd settle for comfortably off.'

'You were?'

'Well...' She gestured to the view before them. 'Not filthy rich, no. But my grandmother died and left me and my mother a sizeable inheritance.'

'Which you... don't have now?'

'Nope.'

He rested his chin on her shoulder. 'What happened?'

'My ex happened.'

'*Oh.*'

Oh, *indeed*. Kelsey cringed whenever she thought about it.

'He... stole it?'

If only. Kelsey wouldn't have felt like such an idiot then. 'No... I gave it to him willingly.' And that's why it really hurt. Sure, he ran off with it, but she'd handed it over to him without hesitation.

Gullibly, naively, trustingly.

Ari didn't say anything. But his arms tightened around her a little more as if encouraging her to tell her whole sorry tale. Kelsey hated rehashing it, but wrapped up with him like this, far away on the other side of the world, Australia and all that happened seemed a very distant memory.

And he'd confided in her about his wife.

'He was a con artist with a get-rich-quick scheme. And I was young and in love. I thought he was a tech genius who was going to be the next Steve Jobs and I wanted to support him, so he could fly to those dizzying heights.'

'So you gave him your money.'

'Yep. Between my mother and I, we handed over half a mil.'

He winced. 'Ouch.'

'Yeah. I didn't do it to get rich, although he'd certainly implied that I would. I did it because I loved him. He was funny and charming and wanted to take care of us. Like my father had done before he'd died.'

That was what probably stung the most – not that he took off with their money but that he'd fooled her into believing he actually loved her. Sure, she'd been young when she'd met him – nineteen – and he'd been almost eight years older, but she'd never been an idiot. And they'd been in a relationship for a year before she'd offered him the money.

Clearly Eric had been in it for the long game.

'It wouldn't have been so bad if it had been just me, but my mum losing her money too…'

He'd refused her mother's money to start with but when she'd insisted several times, he'd caved magnanimously.

Fucking. Bastard.

'My mother had just been diagnosed with a degenerative eye condition at the time and we knew she'd slowly go blind over the next ten years. But that didn't seem to matter to Eric.'

'Did you report him to the police?'

'Of course. It wasn't his first rodeo, though. There's a warrant out for his arrest but we aren't holding our breath. And with my mother's health situation we knew we didn't have time to sit around and lick our wounds. We decided his greed wasn't going to keep us from our dreams so I dropped out of university and got a job with the Ōceanós Line with the goal to save as much money as I could for as long as I could to set us up for when mum becomes more dependent.'

'You're not exactly paid a fortune, though, right?'

'Well, no, but my salary has increased year on year, the conversion rate is in my favour, the tips are excellent and with absolutely nothing to spend my money on I can save most of it. One more contract after this and I'm calling it quits.'

'Because of your mother's sight?'

'Yes. She's lost about 50 per cent of her vision in each eye now. She can still work in a reduced capacity so she's relatively independent, but she can't drive and they expect her eyesight to decrease more rapidly over the next few years. Plus, we'll have enough money for a sizeable deposit and it's important we're settled and established with the house modified and supports in place while she still has useable eyesight.'

He didn't say anything for a while but his lips brushed her skin again, and Kelsey shut her eyes and let her head flop back against his big, hard shoulder. It felt so good here in the circle of his arms.

'I'm sorry,' he murmured quietly. 'About your mother's sight. That must be tough for you both.'

Kelsey's eyes fluttered open. It had been a devastating diagnosis eight years ago. But her mother had always been pragmatic. She'd picked herself up after becoming a widow at thirty-one and she hadn't let impending blindness set her back for long either. 'It was. But we adjusted.'

'Is it hereditary?'

'Yes. Although there isn't a family history that we know about. But... I'm lucky. I've been tested and got the all-clear.'

His arms tightened again and Kelsey snuggled in close to him, aware of the press of his cock against her buttocks. Even flaccid it was an impressive part of his anatomy.

'I'm also sorry about your *malaka* ex. Is he why you're still single?'

'Mostly. It's hard to trust men after what he did and I can't go through that again. They all get judged through an Eric lens now but even then, I don't allow myself to get close just in case one slips through the radar.'

Except for Ari. In seven years she'd let him closer than any man and she'd known him for five days. *Five days*. That should be terrifying her but there was too much bliss here in this bubble right now to go there.

'But he's not the only reason?'

'No.'

A light breeze danced across her sun-kissed skin and she turned in his arms, settling her back against the wall tiles as she snaked her legs around his waist, jamming his not-so-flaccid-any more cock between them. He shut his eyes as she wiggled a little.

His hair was starting to dry and get springy on top, and the sun had deepened the bronze of his skin, emphasising the dark dots of stubble prickling his jaw. His hands slid to her hips, his eyes opening to rest on the buoyant float of her breasts, her nipples putting on a blatantly sexual display.

Her wiggling turned to rubbing and was about to become grinding. She just couldn't get enough of this man. But Ari obviously wanted to talk. He clamped down tight on her hips to stop her squirming and captured her gaze.

'You were saying?'

His hands were remarkably proficient in their hold and Kelsey gave up trying to create some friction.

'Cruise life isn't exactly conducive to permanent relationships,' she said. 'Long absences away from loved ones make it difficult, which is why there's a huge hook-up culture amongst staff.'

'But you could get involved with another crew member, right? On the same ship?'

'Sure. But there's no guarantee you'll both stay on the same ship which makes getting serious difficult and, I don't know if you've noticed this or not, but the *Hellenic* is like the United Nations. The crew hail from all around the world, which means that eventually, if you *do* become serious with someone who lives in a different country to you, there'll be all those challenges and choices to make as well.'

'You don't think something like that could work?'

He seemed serious all of a sudden. Maybe he was thinking about his wife, about how they'd made their cross-culture marriage work. About the value it had brought to his life, despite the pain.

'I'm sure it can and does,' Kelsey said. She didn't want to diminish anyone devoted to making relationships work. 'If both parties are committed. But I'm committed to going back home to Australia. To my mother. She's going to need me more and more and *that's* my priority. Cruising has only ever been a means to an end for me. And why,' she said with a little smile, trying to rub against him again, 'the hook-up scene is more my style.'

His hands held her firm but she didn't miss the way his eyes glazed over a little, or the very definite, albeit brief, drop of his gaze to the shift of her breasts in the water.

'So you're just using me, huh?' he said as he ground against her this time.

Kelsey grinned as his cock hardened between her folds. 'I'm trying my best.'

Then she leaned in and kissed him, gasping as he entered her, giving herself up to the sun and the water and the potency of his possession.

* * *

By four o'clock, Kelsey was dressed and standing at the door with Ari indulging in lazy goodbye kisses. It had been a glorious day – a day that would live in her memory forever – but all good things came to an end.

Including this relationship – or whatever the hell it was. They'd agreed this was it, their final hurrah. But that didn't stop her wanting to linger.

'I got you something,' Ari said when they finally parted, pulling a small beribboned box from his pocket.

Kelsey frowned as she stared at the offering in his hand, which was obviously jewellery of some description. 'You didn't have to get me anything.'

'I know.' He smiled and damn if that smile didn't do funny things to her tummy. She'd never had a problem with goodbyes where men were concerned, but Ari was proving to be the exception. 'I wanted to.'

Her hand shook a little as she took the box. She should refuse but she was curious. Untying the ribbon, she flipped the box open to discover a beautiful Greek *mati* – evil eye – bead attached to a silver chain.

A black dot stared out at her from the centre of the blue glass bead. Kelsey had seen a lot of this type of jewellery over the last seven years. Most of it was the cheap and gawdy stuff they sold in the tourists' haunts.

But this was the real deal from a bona fide jeweller. Everything about it screamed class, from the fine silver chain to the luminescence of the bead to the exquisite polished finish.

She'd bet this cost more than a couple of euros.

'A little something to remember Mykonos,' Ari said as her finger stroked the surface of the eye.

Kelsey glanced at him and smiled. 'If you think I'm going to forget anything about today, you're crazy.'

He returned the smile. 'Here.' He reached for the box. 'Let me.'

She really should refuse but it was such a lovely gesture, and before she could knock it back he was taking it from her hands, removing the necklace from the box. And it was an easy step from there to turn around, face the mirror near the entrance and swoop her hair out of the way so he could secure it around her neck.

'Well?' he said, their gazes meeting in the mirror. 'What do you think?'

It was *divine*. The chain was short and the eye sat just below the hollow at the base of her throat, and Kelsey *loved* it. 'It's beautiful,' she whispered, fingering the eye, 'thank you.'

He smiled and dropped a kiss on the side of her neck. '*You're* beautiful.'

God... this man was good for her ego, and she was going to *miss* him. 'I shall treasure it. But I feel so bad. All I got you was a lousy umbrella.'

He chuckled, his lips nuzzling her skin, spreading goosebumps and tightening her nipples. 'And I shall treasure it.'

Kelsey laughed and then she turned in his arms and hugged him. She would always remember Mykonos.

* * *

The following two days were sea days on their way to Venice and they flew by. Ari spent most of them holed up in his cabin writing his report, which was extensive and which he was presenting at the board meeting in Venice the day after the ship docked.

Being cabin bound was also a good way of avoiding Kelsey. They'd decided Mykonos was it and Ari was fine with the decision. *Perfectly fine.* Kelsey had been some kind of aberration, a crack of sunlight into the bleakness of his life – nothing more. They lived on opposite sides of the planet with very different lives and neither of them was looking for a commitment.

Plus she was very busy with a ship full of passengers. Too busy to smile and chat and flirt. Definitely too busy for one last hook up.

Although *hooking up* wasn't what they'd been doing. Not that there was anything wrong with it if both parties were keen. Hell, Theo almost exclusively hooked up. As did most of his cousins if the European tabloids were any indication.

Ari had even done it a few times himself – before Talia.

But it hadn't *felt* like that with Kelsey – not even the first time. There'd been something between them from the second she'd served him at the bar on the day of their departure.

A spark. A connection.

And it hadn't been sexual. Or not *just* sexual anyway. It had been... deeper. Beyond the recognition of her as a woman and him as a man. It had been...

The umbrella.

That silly little umbrella. Or the sentiment behind it, anyway. A cheap, tacky bit of fluff that had probably cost less than one lousy cent to produce had dragged him kicking and screaming into the land of the living. Had opened his eyes. To life.

To her.

And he wouldn't be seeing her again after today. They'd made their majestic entrance into the Venetian lagoon an hour ago and passengers who'd had an early breakfast were already disembarking. Ari was all packed to go but he didn't want to leave without seeing her one more time. Even if it was just eyes meeting across a room, he needed to catch a glimpse.

Heading to the dining room, he scanned it, his gaze running over the sparsely populated tables. Obviously, most passengers had decided to eat early and get out into Venice as soon as possible. He couldn't blame them – Venice may be a waterlogged old relic to many but to Ari it was a majestic citadel of inconceivable beauty.

Suddenly, he spotted Kelsey approaching a table with a pot of coffee and his heart leapt. Striding towards her, he seated himself at the empty table next to the one she was serving. When she was done, she turned and spied her newest customer, heading in his direction, faltering only slightly when she realised it was him. She was in her formal uniform which clung in all the right places and his necklace was at her throat.

'Good morning, sir,' she said, a smile fixed on her face but wariness in her gaze. 'Would you like coffee?'

'Yes please,' he said, holding out his cup to be filled.

'Are you eating breakfast, sir?'

'Stay with me in Venice.'

She blinked. Hell – *he* blinked. Ari had *not* been going to say that at all. But then she was wearing his necklace and they were both going to be in Venice together so... why not?

She didn't say anything for a beat or two and a hollow feeling in the pit of Ari's stomach deepened to black hole proportions. *He didn't want this to be it.*

Glancing around, she dropped her voice. '*Ari...*'

'I know,' he conceded quietly, his heart beating like a gong in his chest, wanting this so badly suddenly he could barely breathe. 'I know we agreed to not do this but *you're* in Venice for the next two nights and *I'm* in Venice for the next five. It seems a shame not to take advantage of that.'

He searched her face, her teeth digging into her bottom lip like she was giving it serious consideration. Like she was torn. And Ari wasn't above pushing his advantage.

'Come on, *agápi mou*. It'll be just like Mykonos but better. Two solid days in bed. No early morning interruptions for the breakfast shift. We'll order room service and stay naked. Just you and me in a place where nobody knows us.'

He had the board meeting tomorrow at ten but other than that he had no commitments. He just needed to book some mid-range accommodation somewhere because he was pretty sure staying in the family suite in the Gritti Palace would raise questions.

For the first time in days, a little knot of guilt bunched at the base of his spine. Apart from misleading her about the villa in Mykonos, he'd forgotten that he'd been lying to her all this time. Sure, mostly by omission, but he hadn't been upfront with her and there was no sugarcoating it.

Being incognito for his investigation on the ship was one thing; continuing the deception after his mission was complete was another. Especially now he knew about her ex and how much he'd screwed her ability to trust men.

When she'd told him on Mykonos, Ari's blood had run cold and he'd wanted to track this Eric down and kick his ass. There were no words – not even Greek ones – for men like that.

He didn't want to be another man in her life deceiving her, so if she did agree to stay in Venice with him, Ari knew he had to tell her the truth, as soon as she arrived at his door, before anything else happened between them.

'I... don't know,' she said, her brow furrowed.

'Okay.' Ari knew better than to push and he didn't *want* to be that guy. As unwise as it might be, he wanted to see her again, to spend the next two days with her, but he wanted her to want it too. He wanted her to be as unable to resist the idea of more time together as he was.

He grabbed a nearby napkin and asked for her pen. 'Just think about it.' He wrote the name of a hotel on the napkin. It was a good modest hotel and Ari knew the owner. He handed the pen back with the napkin. 'I'll be here. Just ask for me at the desk. What time do you knock off?'

'Sometime between one and two,' she said, her voice faint like she couldn't quite believe she was even contemplating his proposal.

'Excuse me, miss?'

She turned to the man who had called from the table behind. 'One moment, sir,' she said with a smile.

Turning back to Ari, she pocketed the napkin. 'I'll think about it.'

Ari nodded and prayed like hell that she'd find this crazy pull between them as impossible to resist as he did.

11

Kelsey could not believe she was doing this as she stood in front of Ari's hotel door at two o'clock in the afternoon. She knew it wasn't technically against the rules now. They weren't on board, Ari was no longer a passenger and she was on two days off.

But she was supposed to be severing this connection. There was no point letting it blossom any more. Yet here she was at his door, a bag of fresh, crumbly *spumiglie* in one hand and a stupid yellow cocktail umbrella in the other, ready to dig herself in a little deeper.

God... she should go. She should just *go* – walk away now before another two days of fun and laughter and rolling around in the sheets with Ari made it harder to keep her focus. She went to turn away but the door opened abruptly, and he was standing there in a T-shirt and cargo shorts and her heart gave a crazy lurch.

He smiled at her then in a slow, lazy way that had other parts, significantly lower, lurching. 'You came.' He placed a hand up high on the door frame as if he knew how skittish she was and didn't want to go too hard too soon.

'I did.' Damn it, she was here. Time to own it. 'And I came bearing gifts this time.' She held up the cocktail umbrella, which he took with a smile. 'And some food.' She thrust the brown paper bag at his chest.

He removed his hand from the door frame, opening the packet and peering inside. 'Ah... *spumiglie.*'

God, he sounded so... Greek when pronouncing non-English words, his very English accent segueing into something far richer. He stuck his nose in the packet and inhaled before glancing at her and saying with a smile, 'My second favourite thing to eat.'

Every erogenous zone in her body fizzed at the innuendo and Kelsey's pulse hammered like crazy. She *wanted* him. She *missed* him. It might only have been five hours since she'd seen Ari, but it felt like five days.

She was utterly, tragically lost.

Still smiling, he stepped closer, his hand gliding onto her hip, urging her nearer, and when their bodies were pressed together he kissed her long and slow. All thoughts of 'after Venice' fled as she moaned and clung and went completely boneless.

Long, drugging moments later, he lifted his mouth from hers, his breathing just as heavy, and Kelsey was pleased for the solid press of his body as the ground tilted beneath her feet. His thumb brushed along her bottom lip. 'Come on,' he said, intertwining his fingers with hers and tugging gently, 'let me show you around.'

On rubbery legs, Kelsey followed Ari into the room. It was gorgeous in the way of so many places in Venice that had been built several hundred years ago and had undergone a variety of different internal refits since. The bones were made of stone and marble and exquisite decorative plastering, which somehow managed to blend with fittings and furnishings from Louis XVI through to Art Deco.

The bed was huge in the centre of the room, covered with a rich brocade quilt in autumnal shades of gold and auburn, and Kelsey tried not to be distracted by how many times they might be able to roll over in it as Ari led her to the light flooding in through high windows and the sheer white curtain fluttering in the breeze.

'The balcony overlooks the canal,' he said.

The curtains covered a set of French doors and they stepped out onto a narrow wrought-iron balcony awash in sunshine. There was a small square table against the wall with two chairs and maybe another foot in front of it before the curved wrought-iron balustrades.

It was very Romeo and Juliet.

The sights and the sounds of Venice engulfed Kelsey as she looked down. The canal was busy with water traffic – gondolas and water taxis and vaporetto all chugging along beside each other. The thoroughfares and bridges were teeming with people. Bakeries and restaurants and bars were crammed in beside tourist shops selling Carnival masks and blown glass from Murano. English and Italian and smatterings of other languages drifted on the warm air.

It was a delightful riot of colour and life and humanity.

'I love Venice,' she said, sighing happily. 'There's just something about it that makes my soul sing.'

'Yeah,' he said, smiling at her. 'Me too.'

Kelsey's heart fluttered as everything faded to black. All the noise and colour disappearing until it was just the two of them. 'Thank you for inviting me.'

'Thank you for accepting.' He lifted his hand, brushing the backs of his fingers along her cheekbone, down the side of her face and neck to play with the necklace he'd bought her. 'This looks good on you. I bet it looks even better when it's the only thing you're wearing.'

His gaze flicked to hers and there was a heat and rawness there lighting the fuse on the desire that had been smouldering since he'd kissed her at the door. 'It does.'

Hurrying inside, they were at the bed in seconds. Kelsey wanted Ari so badly she was shaking with the immensity of it.

She lifted to kiss him, but her lips didn't quite reach their target before he placed two fingers against her mouth and said, 'I need to talk to you about something first.'

Kelsey frowned as she lowered her heels to the ground. He looked very serious, very suddenly. 'Is everything okay?'

'Yes, it's fine.' He smiled and sat on the bed, one leg crossed up under him, the other still grounded. He patted the space in front of him and Kelsey joined him, mimicking his pose so they were facing each other.

He reached for her hands and held them loosely in his grip. 'I have a confession to make.'

Oh God. 'Okay.'

Except it wasn't okay. This wasn't Kelsey's first rodeo with a guy who was hiding stuff from her, so her brain automatically went into catastrophe mode. He was married. To multiple women. With multiple children. He was a cult leader/escaped prisoner/hitman. He was on the witness protection programme/a spy/dying.

Her brain was melting down with the possibilities.

'My name is not Ari George.'

There was a long pause while Kelsey let that sink in. 'You're name's not... Aristotle?'

She'd loved that his name was Aristotle. It suited him, so noble and masculine and— *Oh, for fuck's sake, woman. Concentrate.* But it was hard to concentrate with a melting brain. Right now all she was capable of was grabbing random stray thoughts.

He shook his head. 'No, it *is* Aristotle.' He took a deep measured breath. 'Aristotle Callisthenes.'

Kelsey blinked at the immediately familiar name. '*The* Aristotle Callisthenes?'

'Yes.'

'The Aristotle Callisthenes whose family owns the Ōceanós shipping line and are gazillionaires?'

'Yes.'

The Aristotle Callisthenes who was essentially her employer. And she'd been... Kelsey snatched her hands out of his. 'Oh God...'

She'd slept with the boss. *Crap.*

Their times together ran like a film reel through her brain on fast forward. Fuck – she'd *played hooky* from a shift to *blow* the boss.

She'd blown him on his dime.

It seemed so farfetched another person might have asked if this was some kind of sick joke, but Kelsey could tell by the earnest set to his face that this wasn't some reality TV gag.

Suddenly, her skin felt too tight, a hand was squeezing her windpipe and her ribs were like prison bars around her lungs.

Kelsey sorted through a mental inventory of the Callisthenes family members she could vaguely picture thanks to Tiffany's addiction to trashy tabloid magazines. They were a large family and popular with the paparazzi because they were mostly young, very rich and they liked to party.

She'd definitely seen Theo Callisthenes' picture a lot. His manwhore exploits were well documented. But she didn't recall ever seeing one of Ari.

'I don't understand...' She stared at his face – his beautiful unphotographed face – and tried to compute what was going on through the background yammering in her brain. The yammering that was growing louder, that was chanting *He lied to you, he lied to you, he lied to you.*

Just like Eric, just like Eric, just like Eric.

'Was anything you told me the truth?' she asked. And then suddenly she was struck by a horrible thought. 'Oh God... are you even a widower? Or did you just make that up to get my sympathy?'

He recoiled as if she'd struck him, and Kelsey hated herself a little. But goddamn it, that was what happened when someone lied – everything they'd ever said was thrown into doubt.

'Yes,' he said, his jaw tight, his eyes two dark murky pools. 'I *am*. My wife, Talia, died in a car accident three years ago. I may have kept my identity a secret but everything else I told you about me was the truth, Kelsey.'

He reached for her hands, but she leapt off the bed so damn fast it halted him in his tracks. 'Why?' Kelsey clutched at her stomach as a roll of nausea hit. 'Explain to me why you're slumming it pretending to be some... ordinary Joe on one of your own ships and sleeping with your staff. I don't understand.'

'Okay.'

His voice was quiet and calm, which made Kelsey want to scream. *Okay?* What possible explanation could there be for this?

'There have been major issues with the *Hellenic Spirit*. It's losing money and developing a bad reputation. We decided to put someone in undercover to investigate. Theo, my brother...'

Right. Theo Callisthenes, manwhore extraordinaire, was Ari's brother. Well, that figured.

'...Insisted I do it because as chief financial officer—'

'So... you're *not* an accountant then?' she interrupted, her voice laced with the bitterness that dripped like poison down the back of her throat. Another lie?

'I *am* an accountant,' he said. 'I'm just... the company's chief accountant.'

Right. The CF *freaking* O of the Ōceanós cruise liner business. Oh, God... Mykonos. That *hadn't* been his boss's house, had it?

A lump of hysteria rose in her throat and she swallowed hard against it. This would teach her to get above her station again. She'd thought she'd already learned that lesson from Eric but obviously not.

'And do CFOs usually do such dirty work?' she demanded.

'No.' Ari shook his head. 'But the cruise line arm of the company has been my baby. I'd overhauled that entire part of the business the last couple of years so I was the most intimately acquainted with it. And,' he conceded, 'I *did* need a holiday. Plus I'm probably the least well known of the family. So I came on the cruise, incognito, investigated all areas of ship performance and have written a report for the board meeting which is here, in Venice, tomorrow morning.'

Kelsey let the full implications of what Ari had just admitted sink in, her heart getting harder and harder. He'd been conducting an investigation? *Christ.* She thought back to their interactions this past week. Had he asked any leading questions? Had he tried to wheedle information out of her under the guise of conversation?

She'd certainly told him stuff as they'd lain in his bed and on Mykonos. Ship stuff. Anecdotes and gossip and the pros and cons of working on board. Her frustrations and gripes and other stuff too. *Secret* stuff about staff parties and the practical jokes they played on each other.

Had any of that been used?

Just how much of their pillow talk was in the report? Had she unknowingly signed some of her colleagues' pink slips?

Kelsey shoved a hand through her hair. Dread sat like a rattlesnake in her gut. What had she done?

'Did you target me?'

He blinked. *'What?'*

'Did you?' Kelsey repeated, her voice low and dark. 'Did you deliberately set out to seduce me so I would give you information on the ship and the staff?'

'*Absolutely* not.' He stood as if something had bitten his ass. 'The report is completely separate to this.' He pointed between the two of them.

'I told you stuff!' Kelsey yelled, her chest hurting as she dragged in a ragged breath.

'I didn't name *anyone* negatively in the report – apart from Jean Paul.'

'How much other stuff that I told you is in it?'

'Kelsey...' He took a pace towards her, but she took two quick ones back and he stopped abruptly. 'I'm sorry I wasn't totally honest with you. Sorrier than you will ever know. But I *didn't* target you.'

Wasn't totally honest? Kelsey suppressed a bubble of hysterical laughter. How about lying his ass off? And she'd been so bloody *easy*. So damn ripe for what he'd been offering, she'd let him in behind the walls she'd built.

He could stick his apology where the sun didn't shine.

'I want to read it.' She held out her hand.

'It's confidential.'

The simmering anger flared through her system like a spray of petrol on a bonfire. If her eyes could have hissed poison at him, they would have. 'I. Don't. Care.'

Their gazes clashed, their eyes locking in a battle of wills. Kelsey didn't withdraw her hand and after a beat or two, Ari headed for his bag. Unzipping it, he pulled out a folder, removed some loose papers then returned to her side.

'Most of the stuff in here is from my own investigations around the ship.' He placed the unbound report in her palm. 'There are things in the report that you told me that helped me build a more complete picture of what was going on with the ship, but I did *not* deliberately target you for inside information.'

Kelsey's hands shook as she sank onto the edge of the mattress and leafed through the report. It was thorough and extensive. Every little problem with the ship outlined and all the factors explored and taken into account before several recommendations were made.

It was all there. Preferential treatment of wealthier passengers. Sexual harassment of staff. Lax distribution of hand sanitiser. Poor food handling standards. Not following medical protocols.

And a dozen other things as well. Ari hadn't held back.

Kelsey cringed at the euro incident in the report, not surprised at all that Ari had surmised the money had been stolen. He had not, as stated, named any names but he had made a notation that the onboard security cameras were to be consulted.

Which meant Andy would probably be getting the boot.

A spike of guilt needled at her before Kelsey pushed it aside. Andy *had* stolen the money. That was on him.

The hardest part to read was Ari's recommendation in the fraternisation section. She glanced up to find him watching her from the low armchair near the window. 'Immediate dismissal of any staff proven to be fraternising,' she read.

He nodded, his eyes troubled. 'I didn't mean you.'

Kelsey snorted, cocking an eyebrow. What a fucking *hypocrite*. If he couldn't see that was a different form of the preferential treatment he'd been so scathing about then he was blinder than her mother. 'Do as I say, not as I do, Ari?'

The dull flush to his cheeks told her she'd hit her mark.

He shoved a hand through his hair. 'I would never jeopardise your job, not after what we've shared.'

After what we've shared?

Like what? Some bodily fluids and stories of mutual heartbreak? But not what he was really doing on the ship. Or his true identity. Oh no, not that.

'We were *fuck buddies*, Ari.' She flung the cold hard truth at him. She would not be seduced into thinking they'd be anything more. He'd smashed that to smithereens for her, and she wouldn't let him think it, either.

His jaw went tight and she was glad.

She stood, the report slipping from her fingers to the floor, the loose pages scattering like rose petals on a coffin.

Which was fitting given how funereal it felt right now.

She couldn't be here any more. Her heart was too heavy. She couldn't bear to be looking at her best time and her biggest regret and know they were one and the same. It hurt too much.

'I have to go,' she said, turning away from him.

'Please... Kelsey.' He rose from the chair, his voice deep and raw behind her, wrapping around her gut. 'Let me make it up to you. I really am sorry, I never *wanted* for this to happen.'

'What did you picture would happen when you set out to deceive me?' she demanded on a half sob as she whipped around to face him.

He'd moved closer to her and his presence was both balm and irritant. She wanted to reach out and touch him, seek comfort she knew she'd find in that hard, broad chest. If only she didn't also want to rake her nails down its muscular perfection.

'I didn't set out to deliberately deceive you. You were... unexpected. I've not been remotely interested in anyone since Talia and I never expected anything to happen between us. It just... did. But I was undercover—'

'Jesus, Ari,' Kelsey snapped. 'You're a fancy Greek accountant, not on the witness protection programme.'

He sighed and nodded as if even he knew he was being melodramatic. 'I'm sorry. This is my fault for getting you involved. Damn it...' He shoved his hand through his hair. 'You were *never* supposed to know.'

'So why did you tell me?' she said, her voice cracking. Why couldn't he have left her in ignorant bliss?

'Because the investigation is over now and there's no need for secrecy, and I didn't want to spend two more days and nights here with you under false pretences.'

So *he* got to feel better about himself by making *her* feel lousy? 'And I'm supposed to admire you for your sudden honesty?' she said, her lips twisting.

'No.'

Kelsey nodded. *Damn straight.* 'It's too little too late, Ari.'

She had to leave. Hell, she should never have come. She should have left Ari as a perfect glorious memory. Out the corner of her eye she caught a glimpse of the yellow cocktail umbrella sitting on the white pillowcase, its canopy spread and a ball of emotion lodged like a boulder in her throat.

She *had* to leave.

As if sensing her imminent departure, he held out his hand and said, 'Don't go. Stay.'

Kelsey shut her eyes, swallowing against the emotion that was like a cramp in her throat. Pulling in a slow breath, she opened her eyes. 'Ari...'

Damn it – what did he want from her?

'I mean it. *Stay*. Please. Let me make it up to you. Hell, come back to Athens with me, give me another chance.'

Kelsey blinked and even forgot to breathe for a moment or two. '*What?*' Was he serious? 'We're a... *fling*. A cruise fling, Ari. That's it.'

'What if we could be more?'

For a moment, Kelsey wondered if she'd slipped and smacked her head and was having some kind of hallucination. *He'd lied to her.* And she had commitments and responsibilities on the other side of the world. Plus – they'd known each other for a *week*.

'Ari... that's crazy, we barely know each other. Actually' – she fixed him with a pointed glare – 'I don't know you at all.'

'Yes you do, Kelsey.' His voice was deep and gravelly and insistent. 'I might have gone under a different identity but *everything* you saw, *everything* I was when I was with you, is the real me.'

The sincerity in his voice snaked around her bones and Kelsey wanted to believe what he was saying, but how could she trust a word out of his mouth when he *wasn't* some CPA on a much-needed holiday and his family were gazillionaires?

Then it hit her. 'Oh my God.' She shook her head as a surge of incredulity rose like bile in her throat. 'I'm *transition woman!*'

Tiff was right. *Jesus* – how had she not seen this?

For the love of all that was holy, didn't she deserve a guy who wanted to be with her for just her? Not her money, not how good a distraction she could be from other *stuff*?

Ari scowled. 'I don't know what that means.'

Kelsey reached for the chain around at her throat and yanked. The necklace didn't feel like a treasured gift any more – it felt like thirty pieces of silver hanging around her neck. She threw it on the floor at Ari's feet.

'It means,' she said, her voice high and getting higher, 'I'm the woman you use to get over the *big love*. The woman to put you back together again for the *next* big love.'

'*What?*' His brow scrunched in utter rejection. 'That's the most ridiculous thing I have ever heard.'

Kelsey didn't give a flying fuck for Ari's assessment. She was done here. She had to get out. She couldn't do this. Everything was too mixed up and achy inside. She couldn't breathe. She wanted out of here. She wanted to go home.

She wanted her mother.

Ari caught her arm as she stormed past him in the doorway. 'Kelsey. I just want to spend time with you.'

'Yeah, well... I don't want to spend time with you.' Wrenching her arm away, she made a beeline for the door.

'What are you going to do?' he asked as she grabbed the knob.

She stilled. She had no idea but she knew she couldn't stay working for Ōceanós. She wanted nothing to do with Ari or his company. 'I don't know.'

'Can I call you?'

A surge of bile rose up her throat as her knuckles whitened around the knob. He had to be joking. 'Don't call, don't message, don't text. Don't internet stalk me. Don't come and visit.' If she never saw Ari Callisthenes again, it would be too soon. 'You stay on this side of the world and I'll stay on mine.'

'*Kaló taxidi.*'

Kelsey didn't know what he'd said, nor did she care, she just turned the handle and stalked out and didn't stop until she was seated on the nearest vaporetto heading God knew where.

A strangled kind of half sob half laugh rose in her throat as she sat at the bow trying not to cry. She should have known her life was going too well to become complacent. That she was due a bitch slap from the universe, because life wasn't meant to be easy, and how dare she think that things could actually go her way.

It had been eight years since Eric after all.

An image of Ari on Mykonos a few days ago rose in her mind but she quashed it. That man *wasn't* Ari. He was Aristotle *Callisthenes*.

Liar. Bastard. Traitor.

Pretending to be somebody else. Fucking her as *somebody else*. All while taking notes. Reporting back. *God*. She could pick 'em. What an *idiot* she was when it came to men.

She did cry then, jamming her sunglasses on to hide the bitter spring of tears. Somehow this hurt worse than Eric. The betrayal cut deeper. Because she'd thought she was impervious to it now. Armoured against it. That she'd learned from her experience all those years ago.

That she was older and wiser.

How could a guy she'd known for a week hurt her worse than a guy she'd been in love with for a year?

How?

Pushing back against another sob welling in her chest, Kelsey set her jaw. She blinked back the tears and hacked back the rise of helplessness threatening to suffocate her lungs. She would *not* break down over some guy who'd been nothing but life support for a cock. She'd known him for a week. One lousy week.

Nobody fell apart after one week.

She *would* get mad; hell, she'd probably end up plotting a thousand ways to get even – in her sleep.

But she *would not* cry.

12

Ari's head was still a little fuzzy from the migraine he'd slept off last night. They'd been plaguing him a lot since his return two months ago and he was grateful for his dark sunglasses as he stood at the railing of Theo's house and stared out over the Aegean.

Mykonos was heaving with his fellow countrymen from the mainland, all here for the long weekend celebrating one of Greece's most popular holidays – *Agios Pnevmatos*.

But his mind was not on the holidays or the view. His mind was on another day, here. With Kelsey. Lazing around the terrace, laughing and drinking and eating. Cooling off in the pool. Leaning on the infinity edge and staring out over the jewel-like vista.

Kissing and touching.

Playful caresses turning into hot making-out sessions. Making out morphing into frantic joining when the fever grew too big and fierce and a desperate kind of urgency incinerated the slow laziness of the day.

He'd been an idiot with Kelsey. He should never have crossed that line. He should have taken his wallet and shut the door. Or at least manned up and been honest.

Because he was no better than her embezzling ex who had lied to her, stolen from her and then skipped town. She'd taken a leap of faith trusting Ari and he'd gone and done the same thing her ex had done.

He'd lied.

And he loathed himself and what he'd done, which only made the guilt he'd felt since his return even more acute.

Oh my God. I'm transition woman.

Those words still haunted him. He didn't know what the hell he'd been doing with Kelsey but she was *not* transition woman. He'd cop to being a hypocrite over his fraternisation recommendations – God knew he'd felt like the lowest kind of slug writing them – but he wouldn't cop to using her as some kind of *place holder* for some other future woman.

Nor had she been a way to forget his wife. Kelsey had been Kelsey. She'd been fun and bright and happy. She'd been generous and giving. And he'd been into *her* – even when he hadn't wanted to be.

He'd *cared* about her. He still did.

Although God knew what he'd been thinking at that moment he'd implored her to stay. It must have sounded *insane*. But he hadn't been able to bear the thought of her walking away. Of another woman he cared for leaving him.

He didn't… *love* Kelsey because that would be impossible. He'd had his one great love in life. The end. Full stop. But… he hadn't been able to stop thinking about her either.

If she *had* been transition woman as she'd accused, surely forgetting her would be simple? Surely he wouldn't be picking up the phone a dozen times a day to get the ball rolling on tracking her down.

Because he had.

But then her 'you stay on your side of the world and I'll stay on mine' would slap him in the face and he'd put the phone down.

Was it so wrong to want to check on her? She'd quit her job, which had been a shock, and he'd been worrying whether or not she'd been able to buy that cottage. Had she found another job? And if so, where? He knew she hadn't requested a reference from anyone at Ōceanós, because he'd asked.

Did a guy do *that* with transition woman?

'Ari.'

A hand clapped on his back and Ari shot a ghost of a smile at his brother. 'Theo.'

'What are you doing all the way over here when three women with their tongues hanging out await your presence in the pool?'

They were speaking in Greek but his brother still managed to sound like a total *kavliaris* – horn dog – in all four of the languages that could slip off his tongue, smooth as cream. Theo always came to Mykonos with house guests because apparently the entire Callisthenes clan crowding in on the terrace wasn't enough.

'One day some woman is going to bring you to your knees and I hope I'm around to see it.'

Theo threw back his head and laughed. 'Hello, my name is Theo Callisthenes, perhaps we haven't met before?'

Ari shook his head in mock disgust. He knew Theo, in his own emotionally inept way, was just trying to keep Ari together, keep him putting one foot in front of the other. He knew his brother loved him and had been his biggest champion and feistiest protector in the aftermath of Talia's death.

But they were very different, he and Theo. Ari had never been a guy who could just move on to the next woman.

'Theodorus.'

The tinkly, sing-songy voice coming from the pool drifted to them on the breeze and Ari was grateful for the interruption from the blonde. 'You're wanted,' he said.

Theo grinned. 'Always man, always.' He clapped his brother on the back. 'Join us.'

'Maybe later.'

Theo departed and Ari turned back to the view and his thoughts. Kelsey *hadn't* been transition woman. If she had, and if Ari had been a different kind of guy, he'd be all over the single women frolicking in the pool at the moment. But none of them held his interest.

Only Kelsey.

That was who he'd been thinking about since returning from the cruise. Hell, to his shame, he'd barely even thought about Talia.

'Ari.'

It was his grandfather this time, slipping in to stand beside him, shoulder to shoulder. He might be in his eighties, his hair snowy instead of the jet black of Ari's memories, but he still stood tall and strong, his mind as sharp as a steel trap.

Yanis Callisthenes had inherited Ōceanós from *his* grandfather and taken it from a small, ailing line to an international juggernaut.

'Pappou.'

'It's a beautiful day.'

'It is,' Ari agreed.

'Makes a man grateful to be alive. To be surrounded by his family.'

Ari didn't respond. His grandfather didn't expect it. Family was a given.

'You are troubled, *paidí mou*. Thinking about Talia?'

Startled, Ari glanced at his grandfather. He saw his *pappou* most days but they rarely spoke about Talia.

'No.' He sighed. Thinking of Talia would be easier. He blinked at the peculiar thought. When had it become *easier* to think about Talia?

His grandfather turned wise, old, *assessing* eyes on his grandson. 'Ah.' It was a smug kind of *ah*. 'I know that sigh, my boy. It's the sigh men have been sighing for centuries over women.'

Ari turned back to the view, silent for a few moments. 'I... met someone... a couple of months ago.'

He wasn't sure why he was confiding in his *pappou*. Maybe it was the age and wisdom thing, or maybe it was the empathy always lurking in his dark, old eyes. 'That's... good,' his grandfather said, also returning to the view, his words considered, careful.

'Is it?' Ari didn't feel good.

Pappou said nothing for long moments. 'You're in love with her?'

Ari glanced sharply to his right, to the proud cut of his grandfather's jaw. 'No.' Absolutely not. He was done in the love department.

A small smile touched the old man's face, but he kept his eyes on the boat traffic making the most of the glorious summer weather. 'Why not?'

'I've had my turn.'

'Ari, Ari.' His grandfather shook his head. 'You think we only get one go at this?'

Ari didn't have a fucking clue how it all worked. He just knew he'd been one and done a long time ago.

There was more considered silence from his grandfather, and Ari's skin itched waiting for him to continue. Because there was *definitely* more coming. His grandfather just didn't like to be rushed.

'I had a fiancé, when I was twenty. Before your grandmother. Her name was Alenka and she was...' He shook his head and smiled, his eyes fixed on the horizon. 'She was a beauty.'

Ari blinked. *What the hell?* He glanced over his shoulder at his grandmother holding court with the grandkids before turning back to stare at his grandfather.

'It's okay, she knows,' he assured him, patting Ari's hand. 'One day, about two months before we were to marry, Alenka didn't feel well. She had a cough, a sore throat, a bad headache. The light hurt her eyes. A cold, we thought. Maybe the flu. She went to bed. The next day her parents couldn't rouse her and she was rushed to the hospital. Meningitis. Three days later she was dead.'

Ari's stomach almost dropped out of his abdomen. *Theé!* 'Pappou...' He slid a hand onto his grandfather's shoulder. 'I'm so sorry.'

'It's okay.' His grandfather shrugged. 'It was the times. They didn't have the drugs, the expertise they do today.'

'It must have been terrible.' Ari knew intimately how deep and dark were the depths of grief.

'It was. And I thought that was it for me too. But your *yiayia*...' He smiled. 'She came into my life a year later like Thor's hammer and turned it upside down. She wasn't an ethereal beauty like Alenka. She wasn't placid and content to just sit at home and let a man look after her. She was a total ball breaker who knew exactly what she wanted. I thought my life was over, that I could never love again, never laugh again. Not the true deep down belly laugh, you know?'

Ari nodded. He did know. He knew exactly. The kind of laugh Kelsey had drawn out of him.

'I was a fool. I almost passed up fifty-five wonderfully happy years – seven children, thirty grandchildren, eight great-grandchildren – all because I was gun shy. I thought a one-woman man meant one woman forever. But it doesn't.' He shook his head. 'The notion that in a whole world full of people there's only *one* person for everyone is ludicrous. We don't just get one go at this,' he repeated.

'Pappou.' This was different. 'We were together for a week.'

And *together* was stretching it.

His grandfather turned his head, and Ari could feel those old eyes on his profile. 'And how soon did you know you loved Talia?'

Ari didn't answer the old man. He'd fallen for Talia at first sight and they both knew it. Yanis's big gnarly fingers settled over top of Ari's once more.

'Love makes you vulnerable. I know that well. But...' His grandfather squeezed his hand. 'Love is everywhere, Aristotle. You've just got to let it in.'

With one last squeeze, he turned and left, leaving Ari's gut churning. Was his grandfather right? Was it possible to have fallen in love with Kelsey in a week? He knew love at first sight was real – he'd been there, done that. The concept didn't scare him. He just hadn't thought he'd get another turn at a grand love.

But *could* lightning strike twice?

Ari didn't know. But with his pulse throbbing through his head, he knew with sudden and absolute clarity that he had to find out. Turning away from the rail, he picked his way around people with single-minded focus, finally making it inside, the cooler shadows of the interior an instant balm to the residual tension from his headache.

'Aristotle,' his *yiayia* called as he reached the front door. 'Where are you going?'

'Australia,' he said as he opened the door and stepped outside.

* * *

Almost three months post Aristotle *Callisthenes* throwing a bomb into her life, Kelsey had finally reached the stage where she didn't think about him every damn minute of the day.

Maybe only a dozen times a day now.

Who knew? Perhaps by the end of the year she'd have that down to five or ten. And by the time her number was up, maybe she'd have it down to only once a week.

It wasn't because she loved him. Or was *pining* after him. It was because anger burned harder and longer – she already knew that from the Eric debacle. And she was hanging on to it because while it boiled in her gut, she wasn't crying. She'd shed about a million tears over Eric – she would not waste a single one on another lying bastard.

Not that she was angry at *Ari* any more. Ironically, she *could* see that he'd been trapped in a lie of his own making and she *did* believe he hadn't set out to trap or hurt her.

No... she was angry with *herself*.

Angry that she'd let her guard down and trusted a guy again after vowing she wouldn't. Angry that she'd picked wrong again. Angry that she'd brought this disaster down on herself by crossing a line she should never have crossed.

Karma really was a bitch.

But... Kelsey sucked in a deep breath of sweet, sea air and lifted her face to the sun. She had *this*. Her toes in the water, sand on her feet and the Pacific Ocean framed in her windows.

Her and her mother *had* taken their sea change. They *had* moved to Pelican Cove. They *had* bought the cottage – even if they were in more debt than Kelsey had planned and they couldn't afford the modifications yet.

But they were here. In Pelican Cove.

Their new town wasn't one of those trendy weekend café-latte hot spots. It was still a little old and faded around the edges. A relic from the seventies that hadn't yet been *discovered*. One of those secret little places overlooked for shinier places nearby.

Which suited Kelsey just fine. She loved the slow pace, the slightly dented charm, the lack of pretence. And she loved her job at the Pelican's Belly Café. She may not be earning a fortune but they were doing okay.

They were happy.

The light breeze ruffled her hair and she let the natural calm of the scenery wash over her. Things might not have gone exactly to plan but look at what had gone right. She had more time with her mother, a community that had welcomed them with open arms and a lifestyle they'd been dreaming about for years.

She was lucky, *damn it*. She didn't need Ari-*fucking*-Callisthenes.

Reaching the rocks at the end of the sweeping crescent-shaped cove, Kelsey retraced her steps, the golden sand soft and crunchy beneath her feet. She had to get home. Her mother's painting class would be over soon and she was picking her up then heading to work.

She passed the rickety jetty that was more fit for scenery than purpose given how badly decayed it was. There were keep out signs posted the length of it and, on the sandy esplanade pathway opposite, a faded sign announced the community fund for jetty repairs.

A very phallic-looking counter graced the sign indicating the level of funds already raised. It was nowhere near the top despite every chook raffle, sausage sizzle or trivia night in Pelican Cove dedicating the proceeds to the jetty fund.

Secretly, Kelsey thought it was beyond repair and needed knocking down and starting again.

It was a twenty-minute walk along the beach and Kelsey enjoyed every minute, staring out to sea as the water foamed around her feet. Drawing level with the beach access sign that led to their cottage, she left the shoreline and headed for the row of Casuarina trees which separated the beach from the land.

Collecting sand on her feet, Kelsey ducked through the low hang of branches to the path, trying to dodge as many of the hard little cones that had fallen to the ground as possible. Those suckers were hell on bare feet.

Relieved when she stepped onto grass, Kelsey headed straight for the hose, which was mounted on the corner of the house that fronted the street. She'd just about removed all the sand from her feet and legs when an achingly familiar English accent with a slight Greek inflection froze her to the spot.

'*Kalimera*, Kelsey.'

Her heart in her mouth, she glanced up to find Aristotle Callisthenes, *as bold as you please*, standing a few metres away, in a T-shirt that hugged his chest and board shorts that hugged his legs, his wavy hair tousling in the breeze.

Kelsey's knees went a little weak and she was grateful to have the house to lean on as she stared. God... was she *hallucinating*? Had her constant fevered thoughts finally conjured him up?

'Ari?' She felt faint and mildly nauseated. She leaned more heavily and breathed in and out slowly. She would *not* swoon *or* vomit at his feet.

He nodded. 'In the flesh.'

Yes. She could see that. And man, he had *great* flesh.

'You're looking well,' he said.

Kelsey's lips twisted. What he meant was, you're looking well – *considering*. Considering all that had happened. 'Well, we commoners don't have the luxury of wallowing in our misery. We have to pick ourselves up and make a living.'

It was harsh and a little cruel but, right now, she was too flummoxed to check herself. And she didn't *owe* him anything.

He grunted, his mouth grim. 'I guess I deserve that.'

Damn straight he did. 'What are you doing here?'

It was supposed to be a demand but it came out all shaky and breathy, and that really pissed Kelsey off. She needed her anger now. She *really* needed it. Because it was patently freaking obvious to her that she'd gone and done the worst thing possible. She'd fallen in love with the man.

Shit. Damn. *Fuck*.

When he'd been on the other side of the world, it had been easy to fool herself she felt nothing other than some very understandable resentment towards him. But with him here and so close, she could take three steps and touch him. She couldn't deny what her gut, her soul, her *heart* already knew – she was in love with Ari Callisthenes.

Double, triple, *quadruple* fuck.

'I live here now.'

Kelsey blinked. Oh dear Lord – this day was just getting wackier. 'What?' she squeaked. She *actually* squeaked. 'But... what about your job?'

She didn't know where that had come from considering it was way down on the list of *what-the-fuck* questions crowding her mind. Maybe it was just the least fraught?

'All I need is a laptop and an internet connection.'

He shrugged dismissively as if that was all anyone required in life. 'I...

don't understand.' She didn't understand any of it. Her brain seemed to be broken.

'Look... I know I screwed things up between us and that you probably don't trust me, and I don't blame you. But I'm not *that* guy. I'm *not* Eric. And I want a second chance. I've thought about nothing but you in the past few months and I want a chance to make it up to you.'

Oh God. This was all too much. Kelsey was still stuck back at the beginning to unpack the rest. 'Wait... you *live* here?'

He nodded. 'At the caravan park.'

The *caravan park*? Aristotle Callisthenes, Greek *gazillionaire*, was *slumming it* in a caravan park? Sure, it was a great little amenity but... it was no villa on Mykonos.

'I...' Kelsey, vaguely aware the hose was still running and she was now standing in a puddle, shook her head. 'I don't know what to say.'

He shoved his hands in his pockets. 'You don't have to say anything. Not yet. I'm going to go now, let you... absorb it all. I just wanted you to know that you're *not* transition woman and I'm going to stay here until I prove it to you. *Christe*, I'll stay here forever if that's what you want.'

He walked towards her then and Kelsey shrunk closer to the house, but he didn't stop until he was standing in front of her.

Close enough to hear the frantic beat of her heart, surely?

Pulling his hand out of his pocket, he opened a blue cocktail umbrella and handed it over. Blue. The same colour umbrella that had started it all.

'Thank you,' he said, 'thank you for breathing life into me again.'

And then he turned and left, leaving her open-mouthed and confused, standing in a grassy puddle with a cheap paper umbrella.

She *wasn't* transition woman. He wanted a *second chance*. He *lived* here now. He'd live here forever if that's what she wanted.

Hot tears scaled her eyes and streamed down her cheeks. Tears she'd kept in check for three months. But now she *loved* him and he was *living* here.

Goddamn it. *How dare he?* Things like this didn't happen to someone like her. She wasn't Cinderella. How dare he wave ridiculous possibilities in front of her face – *now*.

When she was settled and happy. When she was content with her life and her lot.

How dare he come here and fuck with her head.

* * *

It took about 2.5 seconds for all of Pelican Cove to know about the rich, Greek shipping magnate living at the caravan park. The whole town was alive with gossip and Ari put her right in the centre of it the next day.

Striding into the Pelican's Belly, he looked bronzed and sexy and so damn exotic with his *'Kalimera'* greeting that everyone stopped what they were doing and gaped.

'Oh my,' Janice whispered under her breath as Kelsey glanced up from cursing the ancient coffee machine that had more quirks than evolution.

'Ari.' She glared at him. 'I'm busy. What do you want?'

Janice, the owner of the Pelican's Belly, frowned at Kelsey's rudeness, but Ari just smiled. 'Coffee. Black. Strong. No sugar.'

She tipped a chin at a table by the window. 'Sit.'

He didn't detain her, just took the seat she'd indicated and inspected the view. Janice and the three women in the line behind Ari tracked his path. Kelsey rolled her eyes. She'd barely slept a wink last night knowing he was in town – *for her* – and here he was after a night in a *caravan* looking cool as a freaking cucumber.

Paula was up next and Kelsey served her. 'Hi, Paula, the usual?' The harried woman nodded as Kelsey wrote down the order for a cappuccino. 'How's Jaidyn?'

'He's just gone on the public waiting list for a proper wheelchair with all the bells and whistles. Modifying the car wiped us out. Fingers crossed it won't be too long, but it could be up to two years.'

Jaidyn had been born with cerebral palsy. He couldn't walk or talk but was a happy little boy, always smiling despite the difficulties caused by his disability and the pain of his severe scoliosis. His current wheelchair was a basic model, not the highly specialised, very expensive contraption he needed.

'Still, we're luckier than some,' she said, giving a bright smile and happily standing aside for the next customer.

Kelsey gave a more than willing Janice Ari's drink to take over. He cocked an eyebrow at her across the room, but he chatted pleasantly with Janice, who arrived back rosy cheeked.

'So,' she said, her voice sotto voce. 'He says he's here to woo you.'

'Oh really.' Kelsey threw another glare in his direction.

'He's pretty dreamy.' She nudged Kelsey. 'I'd let him woo me.'

A grunt pushed at Kelsey's vocal cords, but she suppressed it. She didn't know why he was here, but one thing was for sure – rich Greek billionaires *did not* woo small-town Aussie women from buttfuck nowhere. She wasn't that woman on the ship and Pelican Cove was not Mykonos.

They'd been in a bubble and it had well and truly burst.

When he was finished, he brought his cup over and handed her another cocktail umbrella. This one was yellow.

'I give you a month,' she said even as a little corner of her heart melted.

He just smiled and walked away.

* * *

Much to her dismay, the man lasted a month. Then he lasted two. Two months of coming into the café every day, leaving her umbrellas, running into her on the beach or at the grocery store.

But it was worse than that. In two months he'd paid for Jaidyn's wheelchair, had a new coffee machine installed in the café and given the local council the money to erect a completely new jetty.

Not only was he *everywhere* but he was a bloody hero to *everyone*. They'd be throwing him a goddamn parade soon.

Worse still was the *speculation*. About her and Ari. The whispers and the nudges and the *advice*. She'd heard they were even running a book on how long it would take for them to get together at the local pub.

It was madness and it had to stop.

He needed to go back home. She wasn't in the market for a guy or for screwing her life up again. Yeah, she loved him. But she didn't trust herself *or* her instincts any more. And she'd rather be alone the rest of her life than go through another soul-crushing disappointment.

She was done with love. And rich, sexy Greek men could just move along.

13

Ari was on the beach. It was windy and a line of thundery clouds swelled up from the horizon. He'd just completed a meeting with the mayor over the new jetty and was passing time skipping stones before his next meeting.

The Pelican's Belly should open soon, allowing him to grab his coffee fix and be back in time to meet with the head of the company that had been engaged to build the jetty.

Coffee fix... Who was he trying to kid? He was going for his daily Kelsey fix.

It had nearly killed him to take it this slow. He knew she didn't think he'd last. That he'd get sick of the chase and give up. And that was his fault because his actions – his *lying* – had only compounded her trust issues.

So he was taking it slow. Rebuilding her trust. Proving to her he wasn't like Eric. That he didn't want anything from her and he wasn't going to cut and run.

Proving he was a stayer. Proving himself worthy.

He had to *try* anyway. Because she may look at him like whatever they'd shared was dead, but she hadn't asked him to leave either. She hadn't told him to forget it and ordered him back to Greece, and he was clinging to that, hoping it meant *something*.

Like maybe there was still a spark. One he could fan with his patience and his presence and his persistence. Because he'd already lost one great love; he wasn't going to lose another. Not because he hadn't tried hard enough, anyway.

He was here for the long haul. For whatever it took.

'Ari?'

Ari turned at his name and smiled at Gail, Kelsey's mother. They'd already met and spoken on a few different occasions. She'd been cool but polite and Ari was in no doubt Gail knew all the sordid details of his and Kelsey's backstory.

Naturally she was on team Kelsey, which meant he had to woo Gail as well. And he was totally here for that.

'A storm's coming,' she said as she approached with her cane.

'Looks like it,' he agreed.

'I don't usually see you about so early.'

'I'm meeting with the mayor and the builder.' He tipped his chin at the jetty. 'About the new plans.'

Gail smiled. 'You've been very generous.'

Ari shrugged. 'What's the use of having money if you can't spread some joy with it?'

'Plenty wouldn't.'

He grinned. 'They don't know what they're missing.'

Seeing Jaidyn's mother cry with happiness and his father break down had been incredibly humbling. *Not* hearing Kelsey curse as she made coffee was an added bonus.

'You must miss home?' Gail asked. 'It's been a while.'

Ari wasn't sure if this was a test, but he wanted to pass it anyway. 'Home is where the heart is.'

'And your heart is here?'

He nodded. 'It is.'

'You love her?'

'I do.'

Ari hadn't been sure when he'd hightailed it out of Greece. He hadn't even dared to hope. He just knew he had to see Kelsey, had to find out. It had taken him a week to track her down and a couple more weeks to organise and manage his absence, but the second he'd laid eyes on her,

her feet in a puddle, her hair in a messy, windswept ponytail, he'd known.

Like he had with Talia.

It was like all the pieces of his heart that had been ripped apart suddenly clicked back into place.

He was in love with Kelsey.

Ari *knew* what love felt like. He knew the deep, abiding constancy of it, the certainty of it, the rightness of it.

He'd just been too burned, too destroyed by it three years ago to trust its embrace again.

You think we only get one go at this?

His grandfather's question had ripped the blinkers from his eyes and the chains from his heart. He *had* thought that, yes. Despite every well-meaning friend and relative telling him love would come again. Despite the evidence all around him that people loved more than once.

Maybe he'd just needed to hear it from someone who understood grief. Or maybe he'd just been ready to hear it this time.

'You hurt her.'

Ari heaved in a heavy breath. 'I did. And for that I am eternally sorry. But I promise you, Gail, if she gives me a second chance, I will spend the rest of my life making it up to her.'

Gail nodded slowly, her lips pursed. 'She's been hurt before. She doesn't trust easily.'

'I know. And I haven't helped the situation. But... I'm not Eric, Gail.'

Ari didn't want to sound desperate or try and ingratiate himself with Kelsey's mother behind her back. He just wanted to assure Gail that his intentions were honourable.

She nodded slowly. 'I know.'

A wave of relief washed over Ari. He knew what other people thought of him shouldn't matter. But this was Kelsey's mother – the most important person in the life of the woman he loved. Of course it mattered. 'Thank you.'

'Don't make me regret it.'

Ari put his hand on his heart. 'I won't.'

'Shall we go and get coffee?'

Ari smiled. 'An excellent idea.' He held out his elbow like he'd seen Kelsey do, and Gail grabbed hold, following a pace behind.

* * *

Kelsey breathed a sigh of relief as Ari took his coffee, bade everyone goodbye and left. Seeing her mother walk in on his arm had been a real punch to the gut. Kelsey knew he was just assisting her, but they were laughing and chatting like old friends and she'd felt a sudden spike of jealousy at their ease with each other.

She still felt awkward around him, a squall of feelings descending upon her every time he was near. Hot and itchy. Angry and sad. And so damn horny she could barely see straight.

Honestly, the man oozed sex wherever he existed and it was getting harder to deny just how much she wanted to tear his clothes off.

He'd handed over another paper umbrella and smiled at her as he'd left like he knew *exactly* how horny she was, and that made her even itchier. She tossed the umbrella in the rubbish but Janice, as per usual, fished it out. Apparently, her boss had taken a liking to kitschy crap if the number of umbrellas taped to things in the café was any indication.

Janice sighed as they all watched Ari cross the road and greet three men. 'If you don't say yes to that man, I will.'

Three other women in the café said, 'Me too,' in unison.

'And me,' her mother agreed, chiming in just after.

Her *mother*. 'What the hell, Mum?'

'What? I'm not *that* blind. And besides... I like him.'

Kelsey shoved her hands on her hips. 'You liked Eric.'

Her mother opened her mouth to reply but Janice got in ahead of her. 'Honey, it's not like you've got any money the man can steal.'

Kelsey's jaw clenched. She loved living in Pelican Cove, but the disadvantages of being in a small town – like everybody knowing your business – were sometimes glaring.

'Hell, that man doesn't need to steal money,' one of the customers piped up. 'He's been throwing it around ever since he got here.'

Yes, he bloody well had.

Red lashed Kelsey's vision. Okay. *Enough*. This had to end. She whipped her apron off, snatched up the cocktail umbrella and said, 'I'm taking five.'

No one stopped her; in fact, nobody said anything, but Kelsey knew without having to look there'd be several noses pressed to the window of the café as she stalked across the road to the beach.

'Ari,' Kelsey snapped as her feet hit the sand, and she stomped towards the four men standing in a huddle about ten metres from the old jetty. They were peering at what appeared to be architectural plans, but all four heads turned in her direction.

Kelsey wasn't concerned that three guys she'd never seen in her life were going to be bystanders to her fury, but she did make a mental note not to kill Ari in front of witnesses.

'Kelsey?'

Ari excused himself from the group and met her halfway. At least with the wind blowing in from the ocean, his companions might not hear the half dozen F words that were already forming on her tongue. Her mother and everyone at the Pelican's Belly behind her, however, would hear them loud and clear.

'Stop it,' she hissed at Ari as he drew to a halt. 'Just stop it.'

The wind whipped her hair back and plastered her T-shirt against her breasts and, as suspected, snatched her words away. He heard them though; she could tell from the set of his jaw.

'Kelsey.'

His voice was calm and reasoned and the itch under her skin intensified. He looked so goddamn *cool*. But also really freaking hot in his standard Pelican Bay *uniform* of board shorts and T-shirt – fitting him in all the right places.

She wanted to push him down in the sand and *impale* herself on him. *Jesus*. Her hormones were out of control.

'Stuff like this doesn't happen to women like me,' she said, lowering her voice as far as she could and still be heard over the noise of the wind.

He cocked an eyebrow. 'Stuff like what?'

'Like Greek billionaires moving into caravan parks for me. I don't *fit* in to your world, Ari.'

'When we were in Mykonos, you said you could live there.'

Kelsey blinked. Was he mad? 'It was *wishful thinking*.' She yelled this time but... Jesus, was he serious? She'd never in a million years have thought it was possible. 'It was a *fantasy*. Wishing for something and having it actually come true are two very different things.'

'Why not?' he demanded. 'Why can't it happen?'

'Because I'm not fucking Cinderella and this isn't a fairy tale. It's real life.'

'You don't believe in happily ever after?'

After Eric? *No.* And how did *he*, after Talia? 'I believe in *not* punching above my weight. I've already had one guy promise me the world. Promise to make me rich and spoil me with first-class trips and diamonds. I'm perfectly okay with not getting on that train again.'

'Except he was a fraud.' Ari's eyes glittered as he pointed at his chest. 'I'm the real deal.'

Kelsey gave a hysterical laugh. 'Exactly,' she yelled. 'I don't know how to be a rich guy's girlfriend. All I know is how to work hard and scrimp and save. I know how to struggle.'

She wasn't lying. She had no idea how to rub shoulders with the wealthy. And it terrified her.

'Jesus, Kelsey.' Ari shoved his hand through his hair, driving some calm into the wind-blown mass. 'I'm sorry I'm rich. Most women would see that as a plus.'

'Not this woman.'

He smiled grudgingly. 'I've noticed.'

'What if your family thinks I'm some kind of gold digger?'

Surely they cared about her pedigree? Kelsey had googled Talia, and her grandfather had been knighted by the Queen for services to Her Majesty. Her father had been high up in the British intelligence services.

Kelsey's father had been a truck driver.

'My family are going to love you. As much as I do. Because you brought me back to life. And that's all they're going to care about.'

As much as I do. Kelsey blinked, the air in her lungs suddenly as heavy as the sand beneath her feet. *Oh God.* 'You *love* me?'

His hand fell to his side and he took a couple of paces towards her. Kelsey knew she should take two paces back, but her legs wouldn't move.

'Yes,' he said, his voice just above a whisper, but she heard him loud and clear. 'I love you, Kelsey Armitage.'

She shut her eyes, shut him out as her body reeled. It couldn't be true. 'Why?' she demanded, her throat raw as tears threatened.

Why would he fall for her when he could probably have just about any woman in the world?

'I don't know – dopamine, endorphins? Whatever crazy chemical reactions happen in a body when it falls in love. And because you're *you*. But I know this feeing, Kelsey.' He took another pace forward and his hands slid onto her upper arms. 'I've been here before and I know exactly what is. And it's *not* a transition thing. It's the real deal. Don't you remember it too?'

She shook her head. She may have loved Eric, but not like *this*. She'd been nineteen and it had been fun and exciting and, she realised now, totally superficial. She'd been in love with being in love and he'd been dashing and older and he'd picked *her*.

This thing with Ari was bone deep and... *she'd picked him*.

Which was what probably scared her the most. She'd never recover if he suddenly got sick of her quaint peasant charms. And how would it even work? He surely couldn't stay here forever, and she couldn't leave her mother again – not after seven years away and her eyesight deteriorating so rapidly.

Kelsey shrugged out of his hold and his hands slipped away as she took a step back. 'I don't want this, Ari. I'm sorry.' She blinked rapidly to dispel the pressure she could feel building behind her eyes. 'I just don't.'

He stared at her for long moments, his jaw growing tighter. '*Malakies,*' he said. 'I don't think that's true.' His voice was taut with control. 'I think if it was true you would have asked me to leave Pelican Cove two months ago. You know the one word I haven't heard from you, Kelsey?' He gave her a beat before he enlightened her. '*Leave.*'

Kelsey frowned. That couldn't be true, surely? She'd been putting him off and pushing him away since he got here. She must have told him to go. She racked her brain for that memory.

But... she hadn't. *She hadn't asked him to leave.*

'If you don't love me then all you have to do is tell me to leave. Send me away. Because I *won't* – he growled the word – 'do it voluntarily. You want me to leave? Then you have to tell me to go.'

Kelsey's legs trembled as they fought to hold her up. It all seemed so simple – why hadn't she just told him to leave?

Because she didn't want him to. She couldn't even bear the thought. Seeing him every day had been a special kind of hell. But not seeing him every day was going to be worse.

Oh God.

The urge to cry rode her like a demon, but Kelsey hung on to her pride with her fingernails. This was for the best. Pulling in a ragged breath, she fished in her pocket and pulled out the cocktail umbrella, her hands shaking. 'Go,' she whispered, slapping it against his chest. '*Leave.*'

Then she turned on her heel and walked away.

* * *

Kelsey was weary to her bootstraps by the time they shut up the Pelican's Belly for the day. Emotional exhaustion hung around her neck, dragging her down as heavy as the storm clouds overhead. She'd decided to walk home, the weather matching her mood perfectly, the wind cool and welcoming against her too-hot, too-tight skin.

She wished she could shed it. Shed everything from these last few months and become a whole new person. Start again.

Start anew.

Ari would be leaving. If he hadn't already. She'd seen it in his face when he'd goaded her to say the words. And seen it in his eyes when she'd *said* them. And felt it in his stare as she'd turned and walked away.

She took a deep breath. It was okay, she could do it. She *had* been doing it. And this feeling, this ache, got better. Eventually. She just had to get past those first horrible days and weeks and months all over again. Restart the clock on the emotional work she'd already done when she'd first returned to Australia.

It *would* ease. It just took time.

Her head and her heart were so full of turmoil, Kelsey actually strode straight past the access to the cottage and she had to backtrack a little.

Walking through the track between the Casuarina trees, Kelsey made a detour to the hammock tied between two sturdy gum trees in the yard. The threatening rain was holding off and it gave good swing and a great view of the water through the tree trunks.

And it was preferable to going inside and talking to her mother. Sure, she'd been very circumspect and supportive at the café when Kelsey had come back after her confrontation with Ari. But Kelsey had known she was busting to say something and she just didn't want to deal with it right now.

It lasted about five minutes before her phone rang. Kelsey sighed and answered. 'Hi, Mum.'

'Are you on your way home? We need milk.'

'Sorry, just got home. I walked. I'm in the hammock.'

Her mother hung up and Kelsey watched as she came out of the house and picked her way carefully across the grass. She was familiar enough with the yard not to need her cane, but her steps were careful.

'You okay?' her mother asked as she groped for the edge of the hammock.

'Yeah.' Kelsey nodded. 'Or I *will* be, anyway.'

'Oh, darling.' Her mother's hand slid on to her leg. 'I'm sorry.'

Kelsey shrugged. '*Que será, será.*'

Her mother didn't respond for a moment and they were both quiet as a kookaburra laughed in the distance. 'He's not Eric, you know.'

'Yeah.' Kelsey nodded. 'I know.' And she did know.

'Eric left and didn't come back. This guy travelled halfway around the world for you. Stayed for you. Fixed up your town for you. Don't blow something good because of something that happened a long time ago.'

Kelsey rolled her head from side to side. 'It's not that, Mum.'

'Then what is it? You're in love with him. And I know he's in love with you so what's holding you back? And you better not say me.'

'No.' Kelsey glanced at her mother. 'It's not you. But... can you imagine him wanting to live here, with us? Forever?'

'So go and live there.'

'Mum...' Kelsey sighed. 'I'm not going to take off and live in a palace in Greece while you go blind in a tiny cottage with a leaky roof, banging around with your cane.'

Her mother laughed. 'What a delightful picture you paint.'

Kelsey shoved a hand through her hair. 'Sorry, I didn't mean—'

'It's okay, Kels.' Her mother smiled. 'I know what you meant. But I absolutely cannot be a consideration here. All that stuff about where you'll live and what to do with your old blind mum are all bridges that can be crossed. But giving up because of them? Using them as an *excuse*? Kelsey... when did you start believing you didn't deserve to be loved by a man like your dad loved me?'

Hot tears scaled Kelsey's eyes. She didn't remember her dad very well. But she did remember the love. 'But Mum... He's the prince and I'm—'

'Cinderella?' She made a dismissive gesture. 'You know she got the prince, right?'

God no, *if only*. 'No, Mum. I'm the stable mouse who gets turned into a horse. And guess what? It's after midnight.'

Her mother made an impatient noise. 'Do you *love* him, Kelsey?'

She nodded, more miserable than she'd ever been in her life. 'Yes.' Her throat burned with the truth of it.

'Then that's all that matters.' She shook her daughter's leg. 'Kels, don't you know *you're* the author of your own fairy tale? *You* get to write the ending.'

Sniffling, Kelsey glanced at her mother. 'Is it really that simple?'

Her mother smiled at her gently. 'If you want it to be, *yes*. Why not? You were hurt. But so was he. The man lost a *wife* and yet he's still willing to put himself out there again. *For you*.'

A hot rush of love for Ari swelled in Kelsey's chest, twisting and lodging in her throat. He loved her. Ari, who had been through a tragedy far more wounding than her own, loved her. Wanted to be with her.

'I ask again,' her mother said. 'Do. You. Love. Him?'

Kelsey couldn't speak so she nodded, her face threatening to crumple from the emotion. Despite all the pain Ari had been through, he wanted to take the leap. With her.

'Then go.' Her mother patted her leg. 'Write the ending.'

A sudden feeling of absolute certainty descended. Her mother was right. If Ari could take the leap, then surely so could she. She didn't know how it was all going to work but she needed to take the first step.

Scrambling out of the hammock as quickly as it was possible to scramble out of a fabric cocoon, Kelsey dashed away tears.

'I'm going to do it.'

Her mother pulled her in for a hug. 'Good for you.'

'I hope I'm not too late.'

'Then run,' she said. 'Go get your prince.'

* * *

Kelsey was *not* a runner but the tide was going out and the sand was packed hard beneath her feet closer to the water, and she ran as fast as her legs could carry her to the caravan park at the far end of the crescent-shaped beach.

She was desperately afraid it was already too late, so much so she barely even registered the rain starting to fall. What would she do if he wasn't there? Old Kelsey would have taken that as a sign from the universe and left defeated.

This Kelsey, this *running* Kelsey, would get in her car and do that mad romantic movie airport dash if she had to.

Her heart was hammering and she was a sodden mess and seriously out of breath by the time she stumbled through the beach gate into the caravan park. Despite the town not being very big, the van park was a decent size and Kelsey had no idea where to start.

'Ari Callisthenes,' she puffed out to a couple who were drinking wine under the shelter of their canopy.

'Number twelve,' the woman said without hesitation, pointing to the left.

Of course the first person she asked would know. His notoriety was such that even *visitors* to the town knew his name.

Stumbling along to the left, it took Kelsey a few seconds to work out the numbering system but, before she knew it, she was standing outside a small white caravan parked on site twelve. The door was shut and she feared the worst as she bashed on the door and called, 'Ari! *Ari!*'

Bending at the waist and planting her hands on her thighs, Kelsey tried to catch her breath. She was dizzy with exertion and almost sick with dread. She couldn't decide if she wanted to faint or throw up.

When the door opened to reveal Ari mostly naked apart from a towel – of *course* – swooning became the obvious choice.

'Jesus.' Kelsey stood, her entire body flooding with endorphins, pulsing at the sight of him. *He hadn't left.* 'Do you always answer the door in a goddamn towel?'

He stared at her incredulously, his gaze roving over her sodden clothes and her hair hanging in wet strips and plastered to her face beaded with raindrops. 'Kelsey? You're soaked. What are you doing here?'

She didn't say anything for long moments, mostly because she was still out of breath. 'I'm writing the ending to my own fairy tale.'

If her statement confused him, he didn't show it. 'Am I the prince in this fairy tale?' When she nodded, he smiled a little. 'That sounds good.'

It could be. God, *it could be*. But... love didn't erase the practicalities and for better or for worse, life had made Kelsey pragmatic. 'I just... don't know how this works.'

'This?'

'Us.' His smile got bigger at the *us*, but she shook her head. This was important. 'Do we live here, do we live there? I can't just abandon my mother, Ari. We just got set up here and she loves it and its—'

'Kelsey,' he interrupted, 'of course, you and your mum are a package deal. And I don't care where we live. We can live here and I can travel when I need to or we can live in Greece or the UK and your mother can live with us if she wants or only part time if she wants, or we can all go back and forth and live all over the place. I know you're a package deal, Kelsey. I'll take the deal. I *love* you. I *want* the deal.'

Kelsey smiled. She was still out of breath but she didn't feel like she was going to throw up any more.

'I love you too,' she said, and *God*... it felt good to say those words. Like something had let go inside her and she was floating free from everything that had tethered her to a life of practicalities and pragmatism. 'I'm sorry I've been so...'

'Stubborn?'

She gave a half smile. 'I was going for cowardly.'

'It's okay. Good things are always worth the wait.'

His slow grin warmed her all over and for a beat or two they just stood smiling at each other, Kelsey getting wetter and wetter as every little niggle and worry she had about Ari's wealth and how it was going to work between them melted away.

'So...' He cocked an eyebrow. 'I should stop packing?'

She laughed, feeling positively *giddy* now. 'Yes. You should definitely *stop* packing.'

'And you should get out of the rain.'

He held out his hand to her and Kelsey moved on wobbly legs to stand in front of him – that towel knot at eye level. With his other hand, he reached for something on the bench near his hip and produced another cocktail umbrella, offering it to her. 'You ever make love in a caravan?'

Kelsey lost her breath again. *Make love*. She'd never thought of sex as *making love*. But she knew without a doubt she was going to spend the rest of her life making love to Ari. She took the umbrella like it was a sacred offering, her heart practically floating out of her chest.

'Nope,' she said as she placed her hand in his.

'Neither have I.'

And he dragged her inside, shut the door and kissed her.

EPILOGUE
SIX MONTHS LATER…

It was a day for blue, Theo Callisthenes thought. The sky an endless arc of wild blue yonder unblemished by cloud, the sea a cauldron of molten sapphire, the church dome atop its alabaster walls a stunning cobalt.

The colours of the Aegean that ran blue through his veins, that stained his very DNA, were the perfect backdrop for Ari and Kelsey's wedding day.

He watched them now, posing for photographs on the smoothed white-plaster rooftop, the sea a 180-degree vista behind, their future burning brightly ahead. They were the picture of love and happiness, and Theo thanked God that his brother was whole again.

Kelsey had breathed new life into him and there wasn't one Callisthenes here today who didn't adore the ground she walked on. Who hadn't welcomed her and her mother into their family with lifted spirits and grateful hearts.

But it was a different of kind of blue distracting Theo today. The electric blue of a bridesmaid dress that hugged and skimmed, that flowed like mercury over curves that should come with a flashing neon warning sign.

Tiffany. The bride's best friend.

Ari had warned him this morning to stay away, and Theo understood that messing around with his sister-in-law's bestie had the potential to blow up in his face.

But Theo had never been able to resist dynamite.

Swiping two glasses of champagne off a tray being circulated by a waiter, he approached, taking his time, enjoying the view. Her eyes, artfully made up in a deep shimmery-blue shadow, met his as he neared, and he shot her a slow, lazy smile.

'Champagne?' he asked as he drew to a halt.

She eyed him. 'Ari warned me about you.'

Theo chuckled. 'Did he now? What exactly did he say?'

'Something about you being a *kavliaris*?' She raised an eyebrow. 'I believe that means horn dog?'

Grinning, Theo nodded. 'Something like that, yes.'

She plucked the champagne glass out of his hand. 'Good then. Just my type.'

And she clinked her glass to his...

* * *

MORE FROM AMY ANDREWS

Another spicy romance from Amy Andrews, *Breaking the Ice*, is available to order now here:
www.mybook.to/BreakingIceBackAd

ACKNOWLEDGEMENTS

I hope you enjoyed *Undercover Billionaire*. My first ever cruise in 2016 was to the Mediterranean and the kernel for Ari and Kelsey's story definitely started back then!

This book has had a convoluted history and I have Clare Connelly, indie guru and all round top chick for encouraging me to keep going with it. She was there right at the start of this book and held my hand through all its ups and downs including a late-night pizza run in New York which was the perfect antidote to one of those "downs". Thank you!

To the Amy Andrews All Stars who read along with me as I crafted the book. A woman couldn't hope for a better cheer squad.

I'd also like to thank and acknowledge several readers who helped me when I put out an SOS during the writing of the book. Thanks to Lynn Brooks who came up with the name Aristotle Callisthenes. And an extra special thanks to Vassiliki Veros and Efthalia Pegios for your combined translation help. Your knowledge of the Greek language – especially those dirty/sexy words – was enormously helpful. Big love to you both.

ABOUT THE AUTHOR

Amy Andrews is an award-winning, USA Today best-selling, Australian author of over ninety contemporary romances.

Sign up to Amy Andrews' mailing list for news, competitions and updates on future books.

Follow Amy on social media here:

facebook.com/AmyAndrewsAuthor
x.com/AmyAndrewsbooks
instagram.com/amyandrewsbooks
tiktok.com/@amyandrewsbooks

ALSO BY AMY ANDREWS

Look What You Made Me Do

Breaking the Ice

Undercover Billionaire

LOVE NOTES
LOVE IN EVERY CHAPTER

WHERE ALL YOUR ROMANCE DREAMS COME TRUE!

THE HOME OF BESTSELLING ROMANCE AND WOMEN'S FICTION

WARNING:
MAY CONTAIN SPICE

SIGN UP TO OUR NEWSLETTER

https://bit.ly/Lovenotesnews

Boldwood

Boldwood Books is an award-winning fiction publishing company seeking out the best stories from around the world.

Find out more at www.boldwoodbooks.com

Join our reader community for brilliant books, competitions and offers!

Follow us
@BoldwoodBooks
@TheBoldBookClub

Sign up to our weekly deals newsletter

https://bit.ly/BoldwoodBNewsletter